WELCOMING COMMITTEE

The five men all wore guns that were worn and well used, and the men themselves were of a type. They were predators, with hungry eyes and cruel mouths and clothes that had seen better days, probably on someone else. Clint didn't doubt that among them they owned nothing that wasn't stolen, probably from the dead.

"Stand aside," Clint said, moving down a step.

"Now, friend, don't make this hard—"

"You're making this hard, friend," Clint said. "You and your compadres here. All you've got to do is stand aside and let us leave."

"We can't do that. We want everything you've got. Just drop your gear—and your money—and then you can pass."

"Not a chance."

"Then you'll die here, and we'll take your money off your—"

Clint knew he couldn't wait for them to make the first move. There were far too many of them. He simply drew and fired, catching them flat-footed. He plugged Clay in the chest . . .

Also from THE GUNSMITH series

And coming next month:

THE NEVADA TIMBER WAR

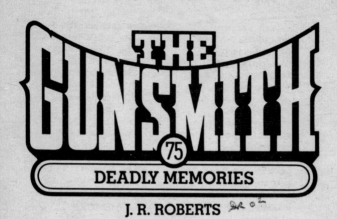

THE GUNSMITH

75

DEADLY MEMORIES

J. R. ROBERTS

JOVE BOOKS, NEW YORK

THE GUNSMITH #75: DEADLY MEMORIES

A Jove Book/published by arrangement with
the author

PRINTING HISTORY
Jove edition / March 1988

ISBN: 0-515-09493-5

Jove Books are published by The Berkley Publishing Group,
200 Madison Avenue, New York, New York 10016.
The name "JOVE" and the "J" logo
are trademarks belonging to Jove Publications, Inc.

PRINTED IN THE UNITED STATES OF AMERICA

10 9 8 7 6 5 4 3 2 1

ONE

The young man called Laramie Jones rode down the main street of Labyrinth, Texas, without really seeing any of the buildings or people around him. He was lost in thought about where he had been the last few years, who he had been with and, most of all, who *he* had been.

"Laramie Jones" was a name he and Gimpy Kane had picked out when they both realized that the young man had lost his memory. Kane had found him bloody and whipped, and had nursed him back to health. They had ridden together ever since—until last month.

During that time, in Rio Malo last year, they had met Clint Adams, the Gunsmith, who had turned out to be the only other man Laramie Jones had met that he liked.[1]

1. THE GUNSMITH #65: SHOWDOWN AT RIO MALO.

Now Gimpy Kane was gone, and Laramie Jones—still a young man, just in his twenties—was alone and, he had to admit, frightened. Faced with the prospect of being alone he had suddenly been struck with the urge to retrace his steps of years ago, to find out who he really was and where he had come from. To do that, however, he would need help, for in almost every possible way imaginable, Laramie Jones was a child, a mere tot in the ways of the world. There was only one man he would ever ask that kind of help from.

Clint Adams, the Gunsmith.

At that moment, Laramie Jones and Rio Malo were the furthest things from the mind of Clint Adams. What occupied his mind was the girl whose head was between his legs. She was devouring his rigid penis with noisy slurps and sucking noises, all of which did nothing to lessen his enjoyment.

Amanda Duckworth was a new girl at Rick Hartman's saloon, and the task of testing out new girls usually fell to Clint—whenever he was in town. On the other hand, if a girl had been hired while he was away, he invariably tried her out—on the house, as it were—just for the sake of his own curiosity.

Such was the case with Amanda.

A buxom blonde in her early twenties, Clint had seen her as soon as he entered Rick's Place, and later that evening they had gone to his room. That was a week ago, and although Clint was thoroughly enjoying Amanda—although it was she who was doing the enjoying at the moment—he had decided that it was time to get moving, again.

DEADLY MEMORIES

But of course, not until Amanda was finished.

Laramie Jones tied up his horse in front of the hotel and entered. The desk clerk looked up and saw a young man who was trail-tired and badly in need of a bath and a room.

"Can I help you?"

"Yes," Laramie said, approaching the desk, "I'm looking for the Gunsmith."

"Who?"

"Clint Adams, the Gunsmith?"

"Hmmm," the clerk said. Laramie Jones recognized the look of suspicion on the man's face.

"No, it's all right," Laramie said. "I'm a friend of his. It's all right to tell me where he is."

"If I knew where he was, mister, I'd tell you,"

Laramie knew the man was lying.

"No, I mean it—" Laramie started, but then stopped. He realized that a man with the reputation of the Gunsmith would not be available to just any jasper who rode into town.

"All right, look," Laramie said, shifting from one foot to the other nervously. "Tell him I'll be at the saloon, waiting for him. Tell him it's very important."

"If I see him, I'll be happy to pass on your message, sir," the clerk said.

"You do that, friend. If I don't hear from him soon, I'll come back to find out why. You understand?"

Nervously, the desk clerk nodded in quick, herky-jerky motions.

As the young man started for the door, the clerk called out, "Hey, what's your name?"

3

"Tell him it's Jones," Laramie called back, "Laramie Jones."

Now that Amanda had done *her* best, it was up to Clint Adams to do his. . . .

He got down between her legs and parted her lips, he tasted her in long, slow licks with his tongue, and then delved deep into her, causing her to lift her plump buttocks up off the bed to meet the pressure of his tongue and lips. He slid his hands beneath her, palming the cushiony cheeks, and pulling her tightly to his face.

When his tongue found her straining clit she erupted into waves of orgasm, and he had to fight to keep his mouth in contact with her. . . .

"Oh, dear," she said moments later.

"What is it?"

"I have to get back to work."

"But we're not done."

She smiled and kissed him.

"There's still tonight."

"There's only tonight, Amanda," he said. "I'll be leaving in the morning."

She pouted and said, "Must you?"

"Yes."

She brightened and said, "But you'll be back."

"Sometime in the future, yes. If you're still here. . . ."

"Yes," she said, putting a hand on his chest, "if I'm still here."

He had never seen such a turnover of personnel in a job as much as he did in the job of saloon girl.

Invariably, when he returned from his travels, there were one or two new girls, and the ones he'd left behind were gone. For that reason he never got emotionally involved with the girls, and he let them know that all he had in mind was for them—*both* of them—to enjoy themselves.

And the girls usually agreed . . . as had Amanda Duckworth.

"All right, then," he said, slapping her well-padded rump, "off to work with you."

"Will you be coming over to the saloon?"

"Soon," he said. "I've got to recover," he added, falling back onto the bed as if exhausted.

"After tonight," she said, "*then* you'll have to recover."

"Is that a threat?" he asked, watching her dress.

"That, my dear, is a promise," she said. "And I always keep my promises."

"Your mother taught you well."

She smiled at him and said, "The things I do best I didn't learn from my mother."

"Well," he said as she left, "I should hope not!"

The clerk saw Amanda leave and knew that Clint was alone in his room now. He didn't want that desperate-looking young man to start searching for him, so he climbed the steps to the second floor and tentatively knocked on the Gunsmith's door.

Laramie Jones had tied up his horse over at the saloon, gone in, and ordered a beer. It was late afternoon, almost evening, and the place was just getting busy, but he managed to find a back table where he sat with his beer and waited.

Clint could tell by the knock that it was not Amanda returning, so he pulled on his pants and answered the door.

"What is it, Jimmy?" he asked the clerk.

"There was a fella here looking for you, Mr. Adams."

"Looking for me?"

The clerk nodded.

"He said he wanted Clint Adams, the Gunsmith."

"What'd he want?"

"He didn't say. He just said that he'd be waiting for you over at the saloon. He was real nervous, too."

"What did he look like?"

"Young fella, maybe twenty-five, real sweaty and dirty from riding hard and long."

"That doesn't help me, Jimmy."

"I'm sorry, Mr. Adams. Would his name help?"

Clint rolled his eyes and said, "It wouldn't hurt."

"He said his name was Jones."

"Just Jones? What's his first name?"

"Uh, jeez, now I can't remember. He said it was the name of a town. Uh, Tucson Jones? No, that ain't it. Waco Jones? No—"

"Was it Laramie Jones?"

"That was it!" the clerk said happily. "Laramie Jones!"

"Well," Clint said, "I'll be damned!"

TWO

When Clint entered the saloon he spotted Laramie Jones right away.

"A friend?" Rick Hartman asked, coming up next to him.

"I'm not sure," Clint said, "but he's certainly an acquaintance."

"He's been sitting there awhile, staring into that same beer. He was real nervous about you, but he seems to have calmed down some."

"What did T. C. tell him?"

"Nothing."

Clint looked around and saw one of Rick's other girls, a doll-like creature named Lila.

"After I sit down, send Lila over with two fresh beers, will you?"

"Sure."

Clint crossed the room to Laramie's table and had to knock on it to get the younger man's attention.

"Got room for one more?"

Laramie looked up and before the recognition dawned on his face, Clint saw a haunted look that should not have existed in the eyes of one so young.

"Clint!"

"Hello, Laramie. I heard you were looking for me."

"Jesus, sit down, will you?" Laramie said, half rising. "Sure, I been looking for you. You got this town sewed up tight? I couldn't get nothing out of the desk clerk at the hotel or the bartender here."

Clint shrugged.

"I spend a lot of time here, and the people watch out for me. Anyway, now that you found me, how's Gimpy?"

The haunted look came back into Laramie's eyes.

"Gimpy's dead, Clint."

"Dead? When?"

"Last month, in Abilene."

"How did he die?"

"He was shot in the back."

Clint's jaw tensed, and it was a good time for Lila to arrive with the beers.

"Clint?

"Hi, Lila. Set them down here. I want you to meet a friend of mine. Laramie Jones, meet Lila."

"Pleased to meet you," Lila said to Laramie.

"Yeah, me too," Laramie mumbled.

Lila smiled at Clint and said, "If you need anything else. . . ."

"I'll call."

After she walked away, Clint leaned forward and said, "Who did it, Laramie?"

"A drifter name of Kenyon. I killed him, but that don't bring Gimpy back."

"No, it doesn't," Clint said, but he was glad the drifter hadn't gotten away with it.

"Clint, Gimpy was all I had, you know? All the family I had after I lost my memory."

"I understand. What can I do for you, Laramie? How can I help? You're welcome to stay as long as you like."

"I . . . can't stay, Clint. I came to ask you. . . ."

"Ask me what?"

"I ain't got no right," Laramie said into his beer.

In spite of what he had told Rick, Clint now said, "Laramie, we're friends, aren't we?"

"Well, sure. . . ."

"Then, you got a favor to ask, you ask it."

"I . . . want to find out who I am, Clint."

"After all this time?"

"It wasn't important, as long as Gimpy was around, but he's gone now . . . and I need to know, all of a sudden. I *don't* know if you can understand—"

"I don't know if I can, either Laramie, but I'll try. What is it you want me to do?"

Laramie looked at Clint with hopeful eyes and said, "I'd like you to come with me."

"Come with you?"

Laramie nodded.

"Help me find out who I am."

"Laramie, what if you don't like what you find out? Remember the conditions Gimpy found you under. Somebody must have a powerful grudge against you."

"Whatever it is, Clint, I've got to find my past, got to know who I really am. Christ, I could have family somewhere. Maybe a wife, some kids . . . I got to know!"

"All right," Clint said, touching the younger man's arm. "Calm down."

"Will you help me?"

"Of course I'll help you, Laramie," Clint said. He'd been thinking it was time to leave anyway. He might as well have someplace in particular to go.

"Really?"

"We'll leave as soon as you like."

"Tomorrow?"

Clint studied Laramie's face and said, "You need a day's rest under you, and I'm sure your horse does, too. We'll leave day after tomorrow, first light."

"All right," Laramie said. "I guess I am tired."

"Now, I'm going to take my beer over to the bar and then I'm going to send that pretty Lila over here again to talk to you. You apologize for the way you treated her before, and she might be real nice to you."

"Clint—"

"You can use the distraction, Laramie."

"But—"

"You came to me for help, right?"

"Right."

"Well, this is my first step in giving you that help."

After a moment Laramie gave Clint a wan grin and said, "Whatever you say, Clint."

Clint went to the bar and sent Lila back to the table, and she went eagerly enough. Watching her and Laramie, Clint hoped Laramie wouldn't start seeing him as a substitute for Gimpy Kane. In finding his past, Laramie also had to find the courage and strength to stand on his own two feet, no matter what he found out.

One thing that had come naturally to Laramie Jones had been sex. It was the one thing that Gimpy Kane had not had to take him by the hand to teach him. Gimpy had taken Laramie to a whorehouse, where an older whore by the unlikely name of Felicity had taken him to a room to see how much he still remembered about sex.

It had only taken a few moments—and the whore's knowing hand on his penis—for Laramie to realize that this, at least, came naturally to him.

Lila was finding out that Laramie Jones knew what he liked and what a woman liked and did not mind letting a woman take her pleasures before his.

"You're a rare man," she said, licking his erect penis lovingly.

"How is that?"

"Most men just throw me down on the bed, poke me and then leave, and I never do get to enjoy myself."

"You enjoy sex?" he asked.

11

"With the right man, of course," she said, taking him firmly in hand, "and you seem to be the right man, Mr. Jones."

"Laramie," he said, "just call me Laramie."

"You're something I don't run across too often in my business, Laramie," she said, flicking her tongue over the swollen head of his penis.

"What's that . . . Lila?" he asked, arching his back.

"A gentleman," she said, "a real gentleman."

As her mouth engulfed him he wondered if he was a gentleman before he became Laramie Jones.

After that thought, he had no room for others, as he realized that Clint Adams had been right.

He needed a distraction—and there was no better kind than this.

"Who was that man I saw you talking to in the saloon?" Amanda asked. It was later in the evening, and she and Clint were back in his bed.

"An old friend."

"He's too young to be an old friend."

"Yes, he is young," Clint said. "He's even younger than you think."

Amanda wondered about that remark, but Clint flipped her onto her back and began nibbling her nipples, and she soon forgot all about Clint Adams' old, young friend.

THREE

Three weeks later Clint Adams and Laramie Jones rode into the small town of Rock River, Wyoming. They still had a few miles to go to reach Laramie, but it was between Rock River and Laramie that Gimpy Kane had first encountered the wounded young man he later came to call "Laramie."

Clint decided that they should begin their search there.

A mile outside of Rock River he called their progress to a halt to speak to Laramie.

"We're looking for two things, Laramie."

"We're looking for my life."

"Ultimately, but here in Rock River, and later in

Laramie itself, we're looking for anyone you know—
or who looks familiar to you—and anyone who knows
you."

"What if somebody knows me and won't admit it?"

"We'll watch their eyes, and if they recognize you,
the surprise should be enough to show. Then, even if
they lie, we'll know."

And so they rode into Rock River with their eyes
wide open, not only seeing the faces of everyone they
passed, but examining them, studying them for the
slightest sign of recognition.

Laramie's concentration had to be twice that of
Clint, because he was also looking for a face that he
would know.

When they reached the livery, they both dismounted
and stood together.

"Anything?" Clint asked.

"I didn't see anyone I knew," Laramie said, "and
I don't think anyone knew me."

"No, I don't think so, either, but then there weren't
all that many people to see. This town looks like it's
on its last legs. Let's get the horses taken care of and
get over to the hotel."

"Can't we go on to Laramie?"

"Not yet. I want to walk you around town, and I
want to find the spot where Gimpy found you."

"I don't know if I can," Laramie said, his voice
quivering.

"Maybe you don't want to," Clint said, "but you
will. It's important."

"All right."

They handed the horses over to the liveryman, who showed no sign of recognizing Laramie Jones. He did, however, recognize the fact that Duke, Clint's huge black gelding, was an exceptional animal, and Clint was satisfied that his big buddy would be well taken care of.

They took their saddlebags and rifles and obtained directions to the hotel.

The hotel was a small, ramshackle wood-frame building that fit in with the rest of the town very well. Rock River looked like a town on the decline—a town that had been on the decline for several years now.

The desk clerk was a young man with a chicken neck and a huge, wet lower lip who showed no signs of recognition when they walked in. His appearance did not inspire confidence.

"Yeah?"

Neither did his manner.

Clint looked behind him at the room slots and saw that most of them had keys in them.

"Two rooms, please."

"Could be expensive," the kid said. "We're pretty full up."

Clint hated stupidity, and for this young clerk to think that he was stupid enough to believe such a statement was the stupidest thing he'd ever heard.

He reached across the desk and grabbed the clerk's shirtfront.

"You hand me two keys, friend, and be quick."

He pushed the boy back, causing him to stagger and knock several keys from their boxes. The clerk

J. R. ROBERTS

hurriedly pulled two keys out and handed them to Clint.

"That'll be—"

"When we're ready to leave, we'll pay what we think this shithouse deserves—and I can tell you now, friend—it isn't going to be much."

The clerk's eyes flicked nervously back and forth between Clint and Laramie, and he wisely decided to keep his mouth shut.

"I don't remember you being that . . . cruel," Laramie said.

"Cruel?" Clint asked. "We've ridden a long way, Laramie—too long a way for an idiot like that to think he can con us. I'm not cruel, I'm just tired."

Laramie decided to stay quiet after that, and they made their way to their rooms.

When Clint entered his room, he almost regretted his decision not to continue on to Laramie. There was dust everywhere, and the mattress on the bed was almost nonexistent.

He dropped his gear off and went next door to Laramie's room, which looked the same.

"Jesus," Clint said in disgust. "I've stayed in ghost towns where the rooms looked better than this."

He walked to the window—which had no glass—and looked out.

"What are we gonna do for something to eat?" Laramie asked.

Clint shuddered.

"I'd be afraid to eat anything in this town," Clint said. "I'll tell you what. Let's take a turn around town, and then we'll mount up and ride out."

16

"It'll be dark soon."

"That's fine with me. I'd rather camp on the trail than stay here."

"All right."

"Let's go, maybe we'll find a general store and buy some coffee. They can't ruin that."

"Or a saloon. I could use a drink."

When they walked through the lobby, Clint noticed that the clerk was gone. He'd always been able to sense trouble, and his senses were singing at the moment. The clerk had obviously intended to cheat them on the rooms, but he wasn't smart enough to make a decision like that on his own. He'd gone to report to whoever gave him his instructions.

"Let's keep alert, Laramie," Clint said. "I smell trouble."

Clint had seen Laramie in action, and he knew that the younger man could handle a gun. He was reasonably sure that they could handle anything that came along.

Anything reasonable, that is.

FOUR

The turn around town did little good. Clint had nearly hit the nail on the head with his remark about ghost towns. Many of the shops and stores had been closed down and boarded up long ago, and the people who were left in town were decidedly unfriendly and were not familiar to Laramie Jones.

They did find a saloon, but there was no bartender, and the bottles behind the bar were covered with layers of dust. The general store had been boarded up a long time ago, like most of the other stores.

"Let's get back to the hotel, get our gear and get out of this dust bowl of a town."

When they entered the hotel the clerk was there,

and he gave them a long, baleful look. Upstairs they retrieved their saddlebags and rifles, and Clint instructed Laramie on how to carry them—saddlebags over his left shoulder, rifle in the crook of the left arm—so that both hands were free—especially their gunhands.

"Expecting trouble?" Laramie asked.

"Lots of it."

When they got downstairs, there was lots of it waiting for them. The clerk was behind the desk with a smirk on his face, and there were five men standing between Clint, Laramie and the way out.

Laramie had stepped off the stairs, and Clint was still two steps up when they stopped. The five men all wore guns that were worn and well used, and the men themselves were of a type. They were predators, with hungry eyes and cruel mouths, and clothes that had seen better days—probably on someone else. Clint didn't doubt that among them they owned nothing that wasn't stolen, probably from the dead.

"Can we help you boys?" Clint asked.

"Dell, here, says you fellas refuse to pay for your rooms," one man said.

Clint assumed that Dell was the desk clerk.

"He tells you wrong."

"You callin' me a liar?" Dell shouted, sticking his ugly lower lip out.

"I am."

"You hear that, Clay—"

"Shut up, Dell!" the man called Clay said. He was apparently the spokesman for the group—a tall, lean man in his late thirties.

"We didn't refuse to pay," Clint said. "We said we'd pay what it was worth, but that doesn't matter now."

"Why is that?" Clay asked.

"Because we're not using the rooms. We're leaving."

"But you already used the rooms," Clay said. "You just came down from them."

"We haven't used them."

"You used them, and you'll pay."

Clint stared at Clay and asked, "How much did you have in mind?"

"We only rent rooms for a week, minimum."

"Is that so?"

"You'll have to pay for a week—each."

"Afraid we can't do that."

"Why not?"

"Because the rooms aren't worth shit, and neither is this town. We're leaving."

"Mister, you ain't got no call to talk like that about our town. We're a little sensitive."

"Stand aside," Clint said, moving down a step.

"Now, friend, don't make this hard—"

"You're making this hard, friend," Clint said. "You and your compadres, here. All you've got to do is stand aside and let us leave."

"We can't do that. We want everything you've got. Just drop your gear—and your money—and then you can pass."

"Not a chance."

"Then you'll die here, and we'll take your money off your—"

Clint knew he couldn't wait for them to make the first move. There were too many of them. He simply drew and fired, catching them flatfooted. He plugged Clay in the chest and another man in the head before Laramie got his gun out and gutshot a third man. The remaining two men grabbed for their guns, but you could see from their faces that they knew they were dead. Clint and Laramie each fired one more time, and then all five men were on the floor, dead.

Clint stepped down the remaining step and walked over to the desk, where the clerk had ducked down out of sight. He reached over, grabbed the boy by the back of the collar and yanked him up and over the desk so that he was sitting on the floor among the bodies.

"Join your friends and learn a lesson. You try to cheat strangers, and you don't know who your dealing with. Next time, you might end up like them."

"Don't kill me, mister!"

"You aren't worth a bullet, son," Clint said, holstering his gun.

Clint and Laramie walked to the door, and then Clint looked back. The boy had not even waited for them to leave but was busy rifling the dead bodies for their belongings.

"Looks like he learned something from his friends," Laramie said.

"Yeah," Clint said, shaking his head. "Something."

FIVE

They camped and Laramie made a pot of coffee.

"That's the last of it," he said.

"That's all right," Clint said. "We'll be in Laramie tomorrow."

"What was that all about, I wonder?" Laramie said, sitting across the fire from Clint.

"What was what all about?"

"That business back at the hotel."

"Just some town toughs trying to rob a couple of strangers," Clint said. "They probably do it all the time."

"Did it all of the time."

"Right. By the way, you moved well there."

"You told me to be alert."

"That reminds me. Don't look into the fire."

"Gimpy taught me that."

"Oh. Well, if I repeat anything that Gimpy already taught you, be sure to tell me."

"It's all right. When we met you, Gimpy told me to be sure and listen closely whenever you spoke."

"He said that?"

Laramie nodded.

"He said there was a lot to be learned from you, so while you're helping me I might as well learn it."

There was bacon in the frying pan on the fire, and Clint took out some hard biscuits.

"Drop them in the grease so they'll soften up," Laramie said and reached for them. Clint had been about to say that and was starting to realize that there were certain basic things an old warhorse like Gimpy Kane would have taught Laramie. He was going to have to keep that in mind.

After dinner Clint said, "We'll take a four-hour watch each and then get moving. We'll be in Laramie for breakfast."

"What are we watching for?"

Clint shrugged.

"Maybe those five at the hotel had some friends. Who knows? It doesn't hurt to be careful."

"I'll take the first watch," Laramie said.

Clint settled down with his head on his saddle and was about to close his eyes when Laramie said, "Clint."

"Yes?"

"Did you notice anything about those five men today?"

"Yes."

"What?"

"They were terrible with a gun."

"Something else."

"Like what?"

"I—I could have sworn that one of them recognized me."

Clint sat up.

"Why didn't you say something at the time?"

"Well, things were happening pretty fast."

"I guess it doesn't do any good to ask which one."

"I guess not."

"It wasn't the one called Clay, was it?"

"No, why?"

"I was watching him, and if it had been him, that would mean I missed it."

"What do we do now?"

Clint laid back down on his saddle and said, "We'll just have to keep looking, but keep something in mind, Laramie."

"What?"

"The next time you think you see someone who recognizes you, let me know right away."

"Even if he's about to try to kill us?"

"Whenever," Clint said, pulling his hat down over his eyes.

Clint woke Laramie at first light, and they saddled

their horses. Neither of them had heard anything through the night, which was just the way Clint liked it. It meant he was possibly being too careful, but that never hurt. He would take being too careful over not being careful enough every time.

Before heading for Laramie, they went in search of the spot where Gimpy Kane had found Laramie Jones.

"It was near a river or stream," Laramie recalled.

After they had ridden a little way, Laramie said, "You know, it could have been north of Laramie instead of south."

"All right," Clint said. "We'll go into town and try looking north tomorrow or later today."

There was a huge difference between Laramie and Rock River. Laramie was teeming with activity, even at this early hour—a town clearly on the rise.

"This bring back any memories?" Clint asked.

Laramie looked around at buildings, at people, and said, "I'm . . . not sure."

"What do you mean you're not sure?"

"Well . . . I have a feeling I might have been here before, but I've had that feeling before."

"Yeah," Clint said glumly, "so have I, in towns where I know I've never been. I guess that doesn't help us much."

"I'll keep looking," Laramie said. "Maybe I can come up with something more specific."

"All right. Let's find a livery, a hotel, and someplace to eat, in that order. After that I want a bath."

Actually, Clint could have used the bath first, but he was starving and simply couldn't wait to eat. He suspected that Laramie felt the same.

They left their horses at the livery—which was three times the size of the one in Rock River, and got directions to the hotel—which was five times the size of the one in Rock River. This one had a well-dressed man in his forties behind the desk, who actually smiled at them as they entered.

"Good morning, gentlemen. Just arrived in Laramie?"

"That's right."

"Welcome, then. Looking for a room, I imagine."

"Right again," Clint said, putting his saddlebags down on the desk and leaning his rifle against it. "Two rooms, actually, if that's no problem."

"No problem at all. We have ample facilities at all times—unless, of course, there's a fair or bazaar in town."

"And there isn't now?"

"No, sir. Would you like rooms overlooking the street?" the man asked.

"Please," Clint said. Maybe it would help Laramie to be able to look down at the street.

Clint signed in for both of them, accepted the keys, and handed one to Laramie.

"You have bath facilities?" Clint asked.

"Of course. I'm sure you gentlemen would like to make use of them before, uh, going into the dining room?"

Clint suddenly became aware of the fact that not

SIX

After they had bathed and changed, they went to the hotel dining room and ate a huge breakfast.

"What's our next move?" Laramie asked.

"The same thing we did in Rock River."

"Not exactly what we did in Rock River, I hope," Laramie said.

"No, just the part where we walked around town to see if you recognized anyone or anyone recognized you."

With breakfast out of the way, they started walking around town. Clint was impressed by what he saw. Laramie was a town that apparently had everything. There were several saloons, every kind of shop imaginable, cafés, even an ice cream emporium. And, of course, the whorehouse. Not only one whorehouse, but two.

"I wonder what they both offer?" Clint said aloud.

"What?"

"The cat houses."

"What do cat houses usually offer, Clint?"

"I mean for there to be two, they must be offering something they think is different from the other."

"Maybe we can find out later."

"You find out and let me know."

"Oh, that's right. I forgot. You never pay."

"No."

"Well, in the interest of setting your mind at ease, I will volunteer to check out both of them."

"Good."

They walked a bit more, and then Clint asked, "Does anything look familiar?"

Laramie frowned, looked around, and said, "I'm afraid not."

"Well, that's not surprising."

"Why's that?"

"Well, look at this town. It's obvious that it's growing, and it's probably changed some since you were last here."

"I don't know," Laramie said, shaking his head. "This almost seems hopeless, Clint. Maybe I've brought you a long way for nothing."

"Let's not give up just yet—" Clint began, but he was cut off by the shot.

They were standing in front of the ice cream emporium when a bullet shattered the glass window behind them.

"Down!" Clint shouted, and they both dropped to the ground behind the horse trough.

There was a second shot, and they kept their heads down until they were reasonably sure that there would not be a third.

Clint brought his head up from behind the horse trough and stared at the rooftops across the street.

"See anything?" Laramie asked.

"No," Clint said. "I don't see anyone, but the shot had to have come from one of the rooftops across the street."

They rose cautiously, and Laramie said, "Now what was that all about?"

"We have two options," Clint said.

"What are they?"

"Either somebody recognized me and was trying to make a name for themselves—"

"By shooting you from ambush?"

"That's the way some people's minds work, Laramie. The other option is, of course, that somebody recognized you."

"And tried to kill me?" Laramie said. "We've only been in town a couple of hours."

"Well, it could be an encouraging sign, Laramie," Clint said. "It's possible that somebody in town recognized you. Now all we have to do is find out who, before they try to kill you—or us—again."

Any intention they might have had of walking away from the incident was spoiled when the owner of the emporium came out, chattering excitedly and calling out for the sheriff. Eventually Clint and Laramie ended up in the sheriff's office.

"You said your name was Laramie?" the sheriff asked.

"That's right," Laramie said, "Laramie Jones."

"Do you come from Laramie, Mr. Jones?"

"No," Laramie said, and did not offer any further explanation of his name.

The sheriff's name was Burton, and judging by how comfortable he seemed to be in his office, Clint judged that he had been the sheriff of Laramie for some time. The man appeared to be in his mid-forties, with gray hair and a pot belly that made him seem older.

"And your name?" he asked Clint.

"Adams, Clint Adams."

"Clint—Adams?" the sheriff asked, with a catch in his throat that indicated that he recognized it. "Um, would either of you know any reason why someone would want to kill you?"

"No," Clint said. "We've only been in town for a few hours."

"I see. Could it be possible that someone . . . uh . . . followed you here?"

"I don't see how or why," Clint said.

"Excuse me, Mr. Adams, but there is a man by the same name who has something of a reputation. You wouldn't, uh, by any chance, um, be him?"

"I suppose I am."

"Then isn't it possible—"

"It's very possible, Sheriff, that someone recognized me and took a shot at me," Clint conceded. "I'm willing to let it go at that."

"It could happen again, Mr. Adams, and next time some innocent bystander might be hurt."

"Are you asking me to leave town, Sheriff?"

"No, sir, I can't honestly do that. You haven't done anything to provoke me into a decision like that."

There seemed to be an unspoken "yet" in the statement, but the sheriff seemed too intimidated by Clint Adams's reputation to speak it aloud.

"And I don't intend to."

"Just exactly how long will you be staying in town, gentlemen?"

"We don't know, exactly," Clint said.

"Well, I'd advise you to be very careful for the remainder of your visit."

"I don't usually have to be told to be careful, Sheriff," Clint said, standing up. Laramie followed his example, and they started for the door.

At the door Clint turned and said, "Excuse me, Sheriff, but have you ever seen my friend before?"

"Your friend? Uh, you mean Mr. Jones here?"

"Yes."

The sheriff frowned and studied Laramie, then said, "No, I can't say that I have. Why?"

"I just thought you looked as if you might have known him. Good day, Sheriff."

"Good day, uh, Mr. Adams."

Outside, Laramie said, "He sure got nervous when he found out who you are."

"That happens to people sometimes."

"Did he know me?"

"I don't think so. I just felt I had to ask."

"You mean he didn't look like he recognized me?"

"No."

During the walk back to the hotel, Laramie said, "What are we going to do now that somebody tried to kill us?"

"Like I said before. We'll just have to try and catch him before he can try again."

"How?"

"That's something we'll have to figure out."

SEVEN

After lunch Clint suggested they ride north of town and try to find the spot where Gimpy Kane had first found Laramie.

"What about the horses? They need rest."

"We'll rent a couple, just to ride out and look."

"Fine with me, but won't we present an inviting target out there?"

"As long as we know that from the start . . ." Clint said.

"I understand. If they try, and miss, maybe we can catch them."

"Them, him, or her," Clint said. "Whoever."

They walked to the livery and rented two horses.

"Is there a stream or lake north of town?" Clint asked the liveryman.

"There's a pretty big stream," the man replied. "Ride north a few miles and then about a mile east, and you'll come to it."

"Thanks very much."

They left town riding north.

About a mile outside of town Laramie said, "Clint?"

"Yup?"

"What happens if my memory just never comes back?"

"I guess you'll have to learn to live with it."

"I thought I had," Laramie said, "and then Gimpy got killed."

"Well, if you learned once, you can learn again."

"I hope so."

"Take my word for it. You can."

Laramie seemed to appreciate the vote of confidence.

"Laramie, have you ever seen a doctor?"

"Gimpy took me to a sawbones after he found me."

"That was for your physical wounds. Was he able to tell you anything about losing your memory?"

"He called it am–am–something—"

"Amnesia?"

"Yeah, that was it. He said he couldn't do anything about it and that I should see a doctor in someplace like New York or San Francisco."

"Were you ever able to see someone?"

"No. After a while it didn't seem so important."

After they judged they had ridden far enough north

they turned east, and after a while came to the large, rapidly running stream.

"Does this look familiar?" Clint asked.

"No . . ." Laramie said, shaking his head. "No, it doesn't. . . ."

"Let's move along. Maybe we'll find a spot that does."

Laramie didn't look very confident, but they directed their horses in the direction that the stream was running.

Every hundred yards or so Clint would say, "Anything?" and Laramie would shake his head.

Finally, however, it was Laramie who called a stop to their progress as he scanned the area intently.

"Something?" Clint said.

"I—I think so. I think—yes, there," Laramie said, urging his horse forward, away from the stream. Clint followed as Laramie rode to and stopped by a large, smooth white stone.

"This is it," Laramie said, dismounting and putting his hands on the rock. "This is it."

"What is it?"

"This is it," Laramie said again. He kept running his hands over the stone's smooth surface, and it was as if he couldn't hear Clint.

Clint put his hand on the younger man's shoulder and asked, "Laramie, what is it?"

Laramie turned and looked at Clint with a look of wonder on his face.

"This is the stone that Gimpy leaned me against when he found me," he said. Turning to look at the stone again he said, "I never thought I'd see it again."

"Does it bring back any other memories?"

A look of great concentration came over Laramie's face as he thought hard, but in the end he had to shake his head.

"No, no, nothing. Just the stone. . . ."

"Stand up, Laramie. Walk around a bit. Something might come back to you."

Laramie did as Clint said, standing straight and walking around the stone in ever-widening circles. Clint stood still and watched.

Laramie closed his eyes at one point as suddenly there was a picture in his head. The figure of a man, and then a man's face, but it was flashing by so quickly that he couldn't grasp it, could not make out the features.

"I'm seeing a man, but I can't make out who it is."

"But it's definitely a man?"

"Yes. . . ."

"Well, that's something," Clint said as Laramie looked at him. "That means that it's not all gone, Laramie. It could all come back at any time."

"Yeah, yeah," Laramie said, nodding his head. "I guess so, Clint. This is great!"

"Yes, it is," Clint said, "but don't try to force it. You'll have to let it come by itself."

They stayed a few more moments, but nothing else developed, so Clint suggested that they head back to town.

They mounted up, sat that way for a moment, and then Laramie said. "All right, I'm ready."

They were halfway back to town when the first shot was fired. It struck Laramie's saddle just behind his butt, and he felt the impact in his legs and buttocks.

"Down!" Clint shouted, launching himself from his horse. Laramie followed his example, hitting the ground just as a bullet struck his horse in the neck.

"Where did it come from?" Laramie called out.

"There!" Clint said, pointing, and as he did there was a shot from another direction.

Clint and Laramie both dropped down as low as they could get and scrambled for cover. Laramie ended up in a culvert, while Clint took cover behind a tree. There were a couple of more shots from both directions, and Clint was finally able to realize two facts.

"Laramie?" he called out so only the other man would hear him.

"What?"

"As far as I can figure, there are two gunmen, no more, no less."

"Right."

"Have you noticed anything else?" Clint asked.

"What?" Laramie asked, ducking his head as three shots rained down on his position.

"Good news," Clint said. "Neither of them is shooting at me."

There were two more shots at Laramie, who shouted, "Is that your idea of good news?"

EIGHT

"Think about it," Clint said. "They're shooting at you, not me. That means they know who you are."

Laramie thought about it, and then said, "Yeah, and they're trying to kill me. What are we supposed to do about that?"

"You're going to have to cover me."

"While you do what?"

"I'll have to move in on one of them."

"Then why don't I move in on the other?"

"Because I need cover when I move, Laramie."

"Let me go."

"No, I've got a better chance."

"I can run faster than you."

"That doesn't matter," Clint said. "As soon as you move they're going to fire on you."

"And they won't shoot at you?"

"You're the one they want. When I move, they might hesitate just long enough for me to get where I'm going."

"Which is where?"

Clint peered out from behind his tree and said, "That's what I'm about to try and figure out."

There was high ground nearby, where somebody with a rifle could hold them down indefinitely. Another possibility was that someone was up a tree, with a bird's eye look at them.

"Laramie!"

"What?"

"Do me a favor?"

"What?"

"Stick your head up."

There was a long moment of silence and then Laramie said, "What?"

"I need to have them fire so I can see where they are. Stick your head up."

"And if they shoot it off, all our problems are solved," Laramie said, but he dutifully stuck his head up, and both gunmen fired at the same time.

"I hope you spotted one of them, because I'm not doing that again."

"See that knoll about seventy yards away?"

"The one with the stand of sycamore?"

"That's the one. That's where one of them is—"

"And the other one?"

"I'm still not sure."

"Well, stick *your* head up and find out."

"That's okay," Clint said, "I only needed to pinpoint one."

"That's seventy yards, at least. Are you just going to run up on him?"

"Do you have a better idea?"

"Yes."

"What?"

"Let's go in the other direction."

"I thought you were the one who wanted to find out who you are!"

"I do!"

"Well, they know," Clint said, "and we're not going to find out from them by running away."

"All right," Laramie said, "just tell me one thing."

"What?"

"What do I do after you get killed?"

"I'm not going to get killed."

"You are if you think you can outrun a bullet."

"Just cover me."

"Without a rifle?"

"Do the best you can."

"Clint, I don't want you to get killed trying to find out who I am."

The two gunmen, apparently becoming impatient, suddenly laid down a barrage of fire.

"They're trying to panic us," Clint said when the firing stopped.

"They're doing a good job as far as I'm concerned," Laramie said, but his voice was strong and steady.

"All right," Clint said, "get ready."

"Jesus—" Laramie said to himself.

Just as Clint was about to bolt from cover, however, they heard the sound of approaching horses—a lot of them.

"Hear that?" Laramie said.

"Yes."

"Help's on the way."

"Help, my ass. They'll scare them away."

Suddenly about nine or ten riders came into view, and Clint stood out from behind his tree. He was peering at the knoll and was sure he saw movement, and then nothing.

The riders spotted him and rode in his direction. He was surprised to see that they were being led by a woman.

"All right, Laramie, you can come out."

"It's safe?"

"I'm sure it is."

Tentatively Laramie stood up, and then when there were no shots, he holstered his gun and moved over next to Clint.

"You fellas having some trouble?"

Clint was surprised to find himself annoyed at the intervention of the group.

"Nothing we couldn't have handled."

The woman took off her hat, revealing short-cropped blond hair, and peered at him. She had a full, womanly figure, and appeared to be somewhere in her thirties.

"We heard the shots, and you sure looked like you could use some help."

"Yeah, well . . ." Clint said, relenting a bit. "I guess you did us a favor."

"You guess?" she asked. "Please, don't let gratitude overwhelm you, mister."

"Adams, my name is Clint Adams."

"Well, Mr. Adams, I've been thanked in a lot nicer ways than this."

"I'm sorry—"

"My name is Susan Bell, Mr. Adams. I have a ranch nearby. My men and I were riding out to check on our herd when we heard the shots. If we interrupted something, I certainly apologize."

"Miss Bell—"

"It's Mrs. Bell, Mr. Adams, and I bid you good day."

She wheeled her horse around viciously, and before he could say another word, she and her men were riding away.

"Well, you made a friend there," Laramie said.

"I guess I reacted wrong."

"That's not all you did," Laramie said.

"What do you mean?"

Laramie pointed over to where his horse had fallen. The animal was obviously dead.

"You fixed it so that one of us has to walk back to town."

Clint looked at Laramie and said, "Well, it was your horse."

"Yeah, but *you're* the one who drove off our help."

Clint, feeling foolish all of a sudden said, "Come on. We'll ride double."

NINE

"Well, well," Clint said.

They were riding into town—sitting double on Clint's rented horse—and Clint spotted all of the horses that were in front of the saloon.

"What?" Laramie asked, his view hidden by Clint's back.

"Looks like our rescuers left us and came into town. I wonder if Mrs. Bell is in the saloon with her men."

"We can find out easily enough."

"*I* can find out," Clint said, correcting him.

"What am I going to be doing?"

"You'll be explaining to the liveryman how you rented a horse from him and then got it killed."

47

"I got it killed?"

"All right, we'll both take the blame. Just dicker him down to a reasonable price for the animal, all right?"

Clint dropped Laramie off at the livery and left him there with the one rented horse. From there he walked to the saloon and entered, looking for Susan Bell.

There were several of her men standing at the bar, while others were split among three tables. A couple of the men at the bar recognized him and turned to face him as he entered.

"Excuse me, but I'm looking for Mrs. Bell."

Three men stepped away from the bar, and once again Clint was able to smell trouble. It was on the faces of the men and in their demeanor.

"What do you want with Mrs. Bell?" one of them asked.

"I'd like to talk to her, apologize—"

"You should apologize," the man said. "You had no call to talk to her the way you did. In fact, I'm thinking maybe we should teach you a lesson. What do you say, boys?"

The two friends who were flanking him nodded their agreement to the proposition, and several men stepped up from their tables. It didn't seem to Clint that all of Mrs. Bell's men felt the same way or were willing to be led astray by one man's bad judgment.

"Why don't you fellas just stand as you were and tell me where I can find your boss."

"Hey, come on, fella," the spokesman said. "We're not gonna hurt you, just bruise you up a little so you remember next time."

"Mister, this kind of horseplay usually ends up with someone getting hurt," Clint warned, "and I can assure you that in this case, it's not going to be me."

"Is that a fact?" the man blustered.

"Believe me," Clint deadpanned. "It is."

Now a couple of the men did not seem so sure that they wanted to go along with the play.

"Come one, boys, this fella's just asking for a lesson."

The spokesman stepped forward two steps before he realized that no one stepped forward with him.

"Fellas—"

"You're all alone, friend," Clint said, taking two steps himself. "What have you got to say for yourself now?"

Clint looked into the man's eyes and saw first that he was unsure, and then that he might just have been foolish enough to try something in order to save face.

"That's enough, Lyle!" a woman's vice lashed out.

Clint didn't look away from the man, but the man—Lyle, if Clint assumed correctly—looked toward the voice and visibly relaxed. Only then did Clint take a look and see Susan Bell standing there, hands on hips.

She moved forward and got between Clint and Lyle, which Clint didn't mind at all. That put her in close proximity to him, and he saw that she was very tall.

"Are you picking on my men, Mr. Adams?"

"On the contrary—"

"Because I'd think that a man like the Gunsmith would have better things to do then pick on a bunch of cowhands."

There was dead silence in the room and then someone repeated, "The Gunsmith?"

At that point, all of Susan Bell's men seemed to realize that a terrible mistake had almost been made. That realization came home, especially to the man Mrs. Bell called "Lyle."

Lyle began to stammer, saying, "I didn't—uh—didn't—mean anything—"

"Sam," Susan Bell said to another man, one of the men who had stayed at his table during the altercation. "Take the men over to the general store and have them start to load the wagon."

"We don't have a wagon," Sam said.

"Mr. Palmer is loaning us one. Do as I say, Sam."

"You're the boss, Mrs. Bell."

Sam—apparently the foreman—rose, picked up his hat, and walked out of the saloon without a word to anyone. One by one, however, the men began to follow him out.

The last man to leave was Lyle, and he once again said aloud, to anyone who would listen, "I didn't mean nothing."

When no one acknowledged his words, he, too, left.

"May I buy you a drink?" Clint asked Susan Bell.

"Why not?"

They walked over to a table and when Susan Bell agreed to a beer, Clint went to the bar to get two.

"You've been talking to the sheriff," Clint said, seating himself across from her.

"How do you know that?"

"He's the only one in town who could have told you who I was."

"Maybe I recognized the name myself."

"But then you would have told your men before this and wouldn't have had to make an announcement."

"Thanks for not killing any of them. I'm short-handed as it is."

Clint bristled.

"I never kill without a reason, Mrs. Bell."

She studied him.

"I get the feeling you were going to apologize to me for your behavior this morning, and now I have to apologize to you for mine. Why don't we just call it even."

"Done."

"Good. Now with that out of the way, can I offer you a job?"

"I'm sorry, but I'm traveling with my friend—"

"I mean both of you."

"No, I'm sorry."

"You already have a job?"

He smiled and said, "I don't need a job, Mrs. Bell."

"Well, that makes you a rare man, Mr. Adams. I can pay you well."

"I'm sorry."

"What if I asked your friend?"

"You'd get the same answer."

She studied him for a moment and then said, "Yes, I suppose I would."

She sipped her beer and then asked, "What was that all about?"

"What was what all about?"

"The shooting that we rode in on."

"I don't know."

"Someone trying to make a name for themselves?"

"I don't know."

"Yes," she said "yes, you do."

"No, I don't."

She sat for a few more moments, then drank some beer and stood up, more than half of it still left in the mug.

"Well, I have to get back to work. It was nice meeting you, Mr. Adams."

"You, too, Mrs. Bell."

He watched her as she walked to the door, a fine figure of a woman wearing a man's clothing, probably doing a man's job.

Where was the man? he wondered.

TEN

"Did you settle up?" Clint asked Laramie when the younger man came in and sat across from him.

"Yes. This mine?" Laramie asked, indicating the beer.

"No, the lady left it."

Laramie picked it up and sipped it.

"It's still cold," he said and finished it. "Want another?"

"Yes."

Laramie went to the bar and got two more beers and brought them back to the table.

"What did the lady have to say?"

"She talked to the sheriff, probably about the shooting, and he told her who I was."

"And?"

"And she offered us a job."

"Us or you?"

"Us."

"Doing what?"

"Doing whatever men do on a ranch, I guess. I told her no."

"Did you tell her why?"

"No. I just told her that we didn't need a job."

"How did she take that?"

"Well."

"She's shorthanded, you know."

"I know, but how do you know?"

"I asked the liveryman about her. He said her husband died several years ago, and she's been struggling to keep her ranch."

"I see."

She reminded Clint of another woman rancher he knew, Beverly Press.[1] She was also running a ranch without a husband.

"She must be a strong woman."

"Liveryman says every town father has proposed to her at one time or another, even the married ones."

"I can see why. She's a very attractive lady."

"Speaking of attractive ladies," Laramie said, "I'm going to finish this beer and catch a nap."

"A nap?"

"Sure. I'm going to check out those whorehouses tonight. I'll need all the rest I can get."

1. THE GUNSMITH #28: THE PANHANDLE SEARCH.

"I'll wake you for dinner."

"Sure."

Laramie finished his beer and left.

Laramie didn't fool Clint. He was going back to his room to try and relax and bring some more memories back, maybe conjure up the face of the man he'd recalled by the stream.

Clint hoped for Laramie's sake that he'd be able to, because the chances were good that it would be the face of his would-be killer.

He knew it was a dream, but that didn't help.

He could still feel the pain of the whip slicing into his flesh: a hot, searing pain, as if the leather were red-hot and burning him, too.

Try as he might he could not get into a position where he could clearly see his tormentor's face. He raised his arms to ward off the bite of the whip and tried to peek between them, but to no avail. It was as if a fog had fallen across the man's face—or was that just part of the dream? When the incident had actually occurred, several years earlier, there had been no fog.

He should be able to identify the man's face.

He should, damn it . . . !

The insistent banging on the door woke him up and he sat upright in bed, covered with perspiration and breathing hard, as if he had just run a mile.

He swung his legs to the floor and hurried to the door to answer it. When he opened it, Clint Adams stepped inside.

"Jesus, what the hell—" Clint said. "I've been banging for a good ten minutes. I was about to shoot the lock off, and then I heard you shout."

"Shout?" Laramie said, wiping the sweat from his face with the palms of his hands. "Must have shouted when I woke up."

"If you were asleep, you sure are a sound sleeper."

"I was having a dream. . . ."

Clint closed the door and looked at Laramie with concern.

"About what?"

"About the man I saw this afternoon, in my mind."

"And?"

"I remember being whipped by him, but in my dream I couldn't get a look at his face."

"And in real life? Back when it happened? You must have seen him then?"

"I can't remember," Laramie said, shaking his head. "I can't. . . ."

"Look, kid, get cleaned up and meet me in the lobby in a half an hour."

"Where are you going?"

"This town must have a doctor. I want to hear what he has to say about amnesia."

Laramie agreed, and Clint left, more determined than ever to help Laramie remember.

If the kid ended up getting killed, at least he should know why.

ELEVEN

The doctor's name was Turner, and he was one of those old-fashioned sawbones who had not kept up on current trends in the medical practice. After they talked, Clint found himself hoping that the growing town of Laramie would do something about getting themselves a new doctor.

"I don't know much about amnesia, Mr. Adams," the doctor said.

"You know what it is."

"Of course I know what it is, young man," the doctor said indignantly. "Just because I don't know all these new-fangled diseases and procedures don't mean that I'm totally ignorant."

"Well, what causes it?"

"A blow to the head usually, or simple shock."

"Is it permanent?"

"Well now, that's a hard one to answer. It could be, and then again, it might not be. It depends on whether or not there's been actual damage to the brain, or just trauma."

"Well, how do you find that out?"

"By waiting, son," the doctor said, peering at Clint over his bifocals, "just by waiting."

"That's all he had to say?" Laramie asked Clint later, while they were having dinner in the hotel dining room.

"No, he did say that sometimes exposure to familiar surroundings can prompt a return of memory."

"How am I supposed to know what's familiar territory if I can't remember it?"

"Well, it worked with the rock."

"Yeah, and what did that get me? A face covered by some kind of fog."

"You can lift the fog, Laramie," Clint said. "I know you can."

Laramie dropped his fork down onto his plate and stood up.

"I appreciate your confidence, Clint," he said, "I just wish I shared it."

"Where are you going?"

"To one of the whorehouses. You said I needed some distrctions, remember?"

"I remember," Clint said. "Go on, I'll see you back at the hotel."

"What will you be doing?"

"I'll see if I can't scare up a poker game."

Laramie nodded, waved, and left. Clint finished his meal in thoughtful silence, wishing he could think of some way to jog Laramie's memory.

TWELVE

When Clint entered the Laramie Saloon it was so crowded he had to elbow his way through the crowds in order to be able to elbow his way up to the bar.

"What will you have?"

"Beer."

When the bartender brought the beer over Clint said, "What are the chances of getting into a poker game?"

The bartender shrugged and merely indicated the crowd.

"If there's one going on, I can't see it," the man said.

Clint turned and peered through the smoke-filled room. There were indeed not one but two poker games going on, but both looked to be for very low stakes, right down to the poor dress codes at the tables.

He turned and called the bartender over.

"What about some private action?"

The bartender eyed Clint for a few moments, then said, "Might be. I'd have to ask."

"So ask."

"I'd need to know who wants in."

"Clint Adams."

The name meant something to the bartender, and quite frankly, this was one time Clint expected it to work in his favor and get him into the game.

Clint only spent money on gambling, which he did not do a whole lot of. Poker was his primary vice when it came to games of chance, and he usually made sure he had enough money on hand to sit in on a game of almost any size. The money came from savings and investments, like the saloon he had a piece of with Buckskin Frank Leslie.[2] Leslie usually sent Clint's cut to the Labyrinth, Texas, bank.

When the bartender returned he said, "You're in luck, sir. There's an open chair."

"I thought there might be."

"Go up the stairs and all the way to the back. Knock on the door and just tell them who you are. They'll let you in."

"Much obliged," Clint said. He finished his beer and set the empty mug down.

"Freshen that for ya?"

2. *THE GUNSMITH #16: BUCKSKINS AND SIX-GUNS.*

"No, thanks. I don't drink when I'm playing poker."

The bartender put his hand on Clint's arm and asked, "Are you any good?"

"Good enough. Why?"

"There's a couple of town fathers up there, think they're special. I'd like to see them get taken."

"You know anything that might help?"

The bartender looked around, then leaned over the bar so only Clint could hear him.

"Now, I ain't never had the money to play in this game, but I've watched once or twice. Mr. Leadbetter—he's the mayor and the banker—he's got a tell that the others may or may not know about. My guess is they don't, because he usually wins."

"Maybe they let him win?"

"Not this bunch."

"So, what's the tell?"

"He straightens himself up in his chair just before he bluffs."

"That's useful to know. Anybody up there playing teams?"

"No, sir. They're all out for themselves."

"Thanks."

"Name's Warren and, Mr. Adams, I'd appreciate you letting me know what comes of this."

"I'll let you know, Warren," Clint said, not knowing if it was the man's first name or his last.

He followed the man's directions, up the stairs and to the end of the hall, where he knocked on a door. It was opened by a large man with an ill-fitting black suit. It fit so badly that Clint could see that the man was wearing a gun in a shoulder rig. Either the jacket was too small, or the gun was too big.

"Name?"

"Adams."

"Come on in."

Clint entered and saw a very large round table in the center of the room with five men seated at it.

"Step right up and take the empty seat, sir," a large florid-faced man said. "We usually have six, but as you can plainly see, we are somewhat shorthanded this evening."

"I appreciate you gents letting a stranger sit in."

The man next to the large man started to say, "Heck, you ain't no—" when he suddenly stopped, as if someone had kicked him beneath the table.

"As long as you've got money, friend, stranger or no, you're welcome in the game."

"Thanks."

"Just know this," the man continued. "That's Jackson who let you in. If we catch you cheating, you'll have to take it up with him."

"You won't catch me," Clint said, and allowed the men to draw their own conclusions from the innocuous remark.

They explained the rules of this particular game to Clint, and the florid-faced man began to deal. Basically anything went, as long as the opening bet was twenty dollars. Check and raise was permitted, "Of course," the man said, and if Clint lost all his money, he was invited to go out and come back when he got some more.

"I think I can handle all of that," Clint said, raking in the cards that were dealt to him for a hand of five-card stud.

They were playing with paper money rather than chips, and Clint set some down on the table in front of him. He noticed in passing that his money had seen considerably more wear than the cash in front of the florid-faced man.

That had to be the banker and mayor: Leadbetter.

THIRTEEN

Introductions were not made. Rather, during the course of the game, the men's names became familiar to Clint and his to them. As he'd surmised, the florid-faced man with all the clean, unwrinkled money was the banker and mayor, Horace C. Leadbetter. The other men were all merchants in town, and apparently—less the missing sixth man—made up the majority of the town council.

"I hope my presence isn't keeping you gentlemen from discussing some urgent business," Clint said at one point.

"This is a poker game, Mr. Adams," Leadbetter replied, "not a blasted town council meeting. Those are held during the day and are rather boring. This game is certainly not boring."

"Not since Adams sat down, anyway," another man said. His name was Tom Champlin, and he owned the general store.

Obviously, he was referring to the fact that Leadbetter—who had been the big winner when Clint sat down—had not fared quite so well since Clint joined the game.

"The night is young, Tom," Leadbetter reminded him.

One of the men at the table was nervous. He was nervous because twice in one day he had tried to kill the man who was traveling with Clint Adams, and he was worried that Adams might recognize him.

The worry was wasted, of course, because neither Adams or the other man had seen him—not this time, anyway. The other man, the one that was now called "Laramie Jones" had seen him, however, several years ago.

The man thought he had left "Laramie Jones" for dead back then. Obviously, he had made a mistake.

He did not intend to make another one.

Laramie Jones was trying to do two separate and opposite things. First of all, he was trying to enjoy the buxom young blonde who was busily working between his legs. She was very skillful and obviously enjoyed what she was doing, but while he was trying to enjoy her, he was also trying to conjure up the face of the faceless man in his dreams.

On one hand, he was with the girl to try and relax, but on the other he couldn't stop turning it over in his mind again and again.

"Mister, there ain't something wrong with you, is there?" the young woman asked.

"No," Laramie said. "I just have a lot on my mind."

"Well," she said, "let's see if we can't take your mind off whatever it is," and she bent to her task with renewed vigor.

Clint disliked Leadbetter. He sat in his chair as if it were a throne and all the other players at the table were his court. He probably ran his town council meetings in just that manner.

He was lying in wait for the slightest sign of the gambler's tell the bartender had tipped him to—if the information was good, and Clint was inclined to believe that it was.

Leadbetter was actually a rather decent card player, although the best pure player of the group was a slickly dressed man in his thirties named Gary Clifton, who also happened to own the Laramie Saloon. The man's mechanics and instincts were excellent. Witness the fact that, despite a horrid streak of luck, he had managed to control his losses.

Finally, during the third hour since Clint joined the game, he saw Mayor Leadbetter suddenly sit up in his chair. Wisler had just dealt out a hand of five-card stud.

"It's up to you, Mr. Adams."

All that was required to open in this game was that

you have five cards in your hand—unlike the variation of the game called "jacks or better" in which you need a pair of jacks or better to open.

Clint did not have a pair of jacks—or a pair of anything—but he figured if the mayor was going to bluff, he might as well beat him to the punch. Other players would certainly drop out, and maybe he'd make a good draw. If not, at least the mayor would not think he could bluff indiscriminately. Besides, he was ahead several hundred dollars at this point.

"I'll open for twenty dollars," Clint said. He had a king and queen of hearts, and three numerical cards that did not match in any way, shape, or form. Once in a blue moon, however, you went with your instincts, and Clint's were urging him on.

"I'm out," the man on his left said. His name was Bob Broome, and he owned the hardware store and had probably owned it for twenty years.

"I call," Bill Knott said. He was a man in his forties who ran the feed and grain.

"I raise fifty," Mayor Leadbetter said forcefully, and the bluff was on.

"I'm out," said Tom Chaplin.

"I call," Gary Clifton said.

"I call," Clint said.

"I'm out," Bill Knott said.

That left Clint, Leadbetter, and Clifton in the game, with cards to come.

"How many cards?" Clifton asked Clint.

"Three," Clint said, holding the king and queen and discarding the rest.

"Mayor?"

"I'll play these, gentlemen," the man said smugly.

"In that case," Clifton said, "the dealer takes two."

The cards dealt out, Clifton looked at Clint and said, "Your play."

"I'll bet into the raiser," Clint said. "Fifty dollars."

A couple of the other men showed their surprise.

"I'm afraid I'll have to raise you back, sir," Leadbetter said. "One hundred dollars."

"Getting steep," Clifton said, although Clint had the feeling the man wasn't worried at all. He watched the saloon owner take an unnecessary look at his cards—the man *always* knew what he had—and then begin counting out money.

"I call," he said, tossing one hundred fifty dollars into the pot, "and raise the same amount," followed by another hundred fifty.

Clint spread his cards and saw to his amazement that he had drawn three more hearts, giving him a king high flush. Leadbetter had stood pat—bluffing, remember—so Clint was not afraid of him. It was Clifton, who had drawn two cards, who concerned him. The man did not strike him as the type to keep an ace kicker with a pair, so he figured to have drawn two cards to three of a kind. He could have a full house, four of a kind, or—if he had not improved his hand—simply three of a kind.

In two out of three of those choices, Clint was a loser.

"I call."

All eyes went to Leadbetter, who had started the

raising. Clint knew that the man had too much ego to let go now.

"Five hundred dollars," the man said.

It had only been the girl's dogged determination that had raised Laramie Jones to the proper heights, and when he exploded in her mouth, all other thoughts fled from his mind.

Now he was lying on his back with the girl astride him, his rigid penis buried deeply inside of her. She was slapping his face playfully with her smooth, firm breasts, and he was trying to catch the nipples in his mouth.

As she brought herself down firmly on him, her insides closed over him like a slick glove, and once again he was able to empty his mind . . . but for how long?

"Excuse me, Horace," Clifton said. "Are you calling my hundred and fifty raise and raising three-fifty, or are you raising me five hundred?"

"I'm putting five hundred into the pot," the man said. "I'm raising you three-fifty."

"Ah," Clifton said. "Well, I'll call."

"So will I," Clint said. He had a feeling his money was going south, but would never have forgiven himself if he let Clifton take the pot from him with three of a kind.

Leadbetter frowned and said, "Beat two pair."

Clifton laid his cards down, showing three aces and a pair of fours.

"Your pot, Clifton," Clint said, tossing his flush into the discards.

"You took a beating in this hand, Horace," Clifton said. He seemed to enjoy rubbing it in. "That'll teach you to bluff."

"The night is young, Clifton," the mayor said through clenched teeth.

He was right, Clint decided. Now even, he still had time to win some money.

FOURTEEN

The game continued but that hand seemed to have been its high point, and it eventually came to an end.

At the end Clint had managed to win a hundred dollars or so, and although it was not a huge sum of money, he had enjoyed the play.

"I have to thank you gentlemen again for allowing me to play," he said as they all stood to leave. "It was an interesting experience."

"Yes, it certainly was," Gary Clifton said. He had turned out to be the big winner.

The mayor, Horace Leadbetter, was in a foul mood because he had lost two hundred dollars.

"Wasn't it interesting, Mayor?" Clifton asked.

"Very. I have to go, gentlemen. See you next time."

The mayor left, along with the others, and as Clint was about to follow them out, Clifton called out to him.

"Would you care for a drink, Mr. Adams?"

Clint checked the time and was surprised to find that it was almost three in the morning.

"You're not still open, are you?"

Clifton smiled.

"It's my place, remember," he said. "I can open it for two thristy men."

"You've got a deal, Mr. Clifton."

"Call me Gary."

"And I'm Clint."

"And now that that's settled, let's go downstairs for that drink."

The man who had twice tried to kill Laramie Jones went home and thought about how easy it would have been to kill Clint Adams at that poker table, but that would not have solved his problem. Laramie Jones would be left alive, and it was Jones who was the danger to him, not Clint Adams. Clint Adams had never seen him before and would not be able to identify him.

Laramie Jones would.

And then again, it might not have been that easy to kill Clint Adams. He was, after all, the Gunsmith.

Gary Clifton and Clint Adams cleaned the inverted chairs off a table and sat with a bottle of whiskey between them.

"What brings you to Laramie, Clint?" Clifton asked.

"Certainly not our little poker game."

"No. I hadn't heard about that until tonight."

"I see. What then?"

Clint shrugged.

"Just passing through."

"On your way to where?"

Clint hesitated, then asked, "Is this why you asked me to stay for a drink? So you could ask me questions?"

Now Clifton shrugged.

"We don't get living legends in town very often. I don't mind telling you that I'm impressed."

"Don't be. There's nothing to be impressed with."

"Oh, I realize that reputations are exaggerated, but there is usually a basis upon which to exaggerate, don't you think?"

"I suppose."

"Even if you've only done half the things you're reputed to have done, you have to admit that's pretty impressive."

"I don't think much about it," Clint said. He put his empty glass down on the table and said, "Thanks for the drink, Gary."

"Leaving so soon?"

"It's late, and I've got things to do tomorrow morning."

"Well, come by tomorrow night."

"Is there another game?"

"No, but bring your friend and I'll buy you both a drink."

"Sure," Clint said. Clifton let him out the front door and locked it behind him. Clint walked back to his hotel wondering how much more inquisitive Clifton

77

would have gotten given the chance.

At the hotel Clint checked with the desk clerk to see if Laramie had gotten in and found that he had. He checked the younger man's door on the way to his room and found it locked. He listened for a few moments but couldn't hear anything. He wondered if Laramie were sleeping peacefully.

He felt the leather of the whip rip open his flesh, and the warmth of the blood as it flowed. He was naked, totally defenseless. He tried to cover up with his arms, but only succeeded in having them cut to ribbons, as well.

The sun was hot, but that had nothing to do with the way his flesh burned. The whip bit into the softer flesh of his buttocks, and he cried out.

He tried to see the man's face, but the sun was directly behind him and he couldn't make it out. Once again he buried his head in his arms and prayed for a quick death, but the man with the whip knew what he was doing. Death would come, but not quickly, and not soon—

Laramie jerked awake and sat upright, his back stiff. He was covered with sweat and found he was holding his breath. He let it out in a great, shuddering blast and then tried to regulate his breathing.

He had left the whorehouse late, after having decided not to spend the night there. The woman he'd been with had been fine for sex, but he'd had no desire to sleep with her. Upon his return to the hotel he had gone immediately to bed, hoping that he was tired enough to fall into a deep, dreamless sleep.

Alas, that had not been the case.

The dream had been the same, except this time instead of fog, the man's face had been protected by intense sunlight.

He touched his back where he still bore the scars from the whip, and he swore he could still feel the burning sensation, as if the scars had opened and the skin still hung there in flaps.

He stood up and walked to the window, cracking it open. He sat there and let the breeze dry the sweat on his body, then closed the window and went back to bed.

He lay awake for a long time, afraid to close his eyes but finally fell asleep.

And dreamed.

FIFTEEN

In the morning Clint went to Laramie's room to wake him, but there was no answer. He went downstairs and found him already having breakfast.

"You're up early after a late night," Clint said, sitting down across from him.

Laramie looked at him and Clint saw how red-rimmed his eyes were, looking as if they had sunk into his head.

"What the hell—"

"I can't go to sleep," Laramie said. "I keep dreaming about the man with the whip, by the stream . . ."

"Do you remember anything?"

"I remember how the whip felt and how my skin

81

burned and how much more it hurt knowing that the cool water of that stream was right there next to me." Laramie got a faraway look in his eyes. "You have no idea how it felt, Clint, being able to hear the water running, knowing how cold it was because I had drunk from it that morning. My skin was on fire, and I couldn't get near the stream—"

"Laramie."

Laramie looked at Clint and his eyes focused.

"Was the man alone? Do you remember that?"

"I don't—wait." He closed his eyes, conjuring up the dream, and then opened them. "I can't tell. I can never see anyone else in the dream, and I can't see the face of the man with the whip."

A waiter came over and took Clint's order for breakfast. Laramie had ordered only coffee and some biscuits, and those were only half eaten.

After the waiter left Laramie said, "This is a waste of time, Clint. Maybe if we leave Laramie I'll stop having the dream."

"The dream is the only link you have with your past, Laramie. You've got to use it."

"How?"

"It's your dream," Clint said. "Control it. Do what you weren't able to do in real life."

"What?"

"Stand up, and see the face of the man with the whip."

"I can't—"

"You couldn't then," Clint said, "but you can now. See, it's only a dream now."

"I'm . . . afraid to go to sleep."

"Wait until tonight. You'll go to sleep and you'll dream, and then you'll see his face. Right now he's stalking us," Clint said. "But once you see his face, it'll be us stalking him."

"We could leave—" Laramie started again, but Clint cut him off.

"I don't think that would do any good, Laramie. If this man is afraid of you—and we can assume that he is—then he'll be afraid to let you leave, because if you do you can always come back."

"Then . . . I don't have any choice?"

"I don't think you ever did, Laramie. Not if you want the truth." Clint hesitated, then leaned forward and asked, "You do still want the truth, don't you?"

Laramie looked into his coffee cup, as if the answer would be there.

"Yes," he said, finally, "I want the truth."

"All right," Clint said. "Then we'll get it."

Clint's breakfast came, and when Laramie saw it he told the waiter to bring him the same thing.

"That's a good sign," Clint said. "Want some of mine?"

"No," Laramie said with a lopsided grin, "I'll wait."

"How did your research go last night?"

"Fine, I suppose."

"Don't be so enthusiastic about it or I might run right over there."

"I guess my heart just wasn't in it."

"When you go to a whorehouse," Clint said, "your heart is the last thing you need."

"What did you do last night?"

Clint told him about the poker game and about meeting the town fathers. Then he told him about being questioned by Gary Clifton.

"He sounds like a very curious man. Maybe I should meet him."

"Well, he invited us to come to the saloon tonight for a drink. I guess we'll do that and you can get a look at him and see if he's familiar. Maybe he'll be the man in your dream."

"For his sake," Laramie said, "he'd better hope that he's not."

SIXTEEN

"I have to talk to you," the man said.

"Come on in," Gary Clifton said.

The man sat across from Clifton, drywashing his hands nervously. Clifton sat at his desk.

"You're not going to tell me that you're the one who took shots at Clint Adams and his friend, are you?"

The man stared at Clifton, then nodded his head and said, "Yes, it was me."

"Are you crazy?" Clifton demanded. "They would have simply passed through and never come back if you had let it alone."

"Not if he had seen me," the other man said. "If he recognizes you—"

"Maybe he won't. Look, Adams said they were passing through, and maybe they are."

"I don't like it," the other man said, "too much coincidence."

"Haven't you ever passed through the same town twice—oh, I forgot. You haven't traveled much, have you?"

"Only during the war."

"And then you came here and settled down—with my help, of course."

"Of course."

"And now you want my help again, right?"

"I need it."

"Well, you wouldn't if you had come and talked to me before going off half-cocked. Who else did you drag into this with you?"

"I just hired a guy to back my play."

"What did you tell him?"

"I didn't tell him anything, Gary—"

"All right, keep it that way. Pay him and get him out of town."

"I already paid him—"

"Well, give him some more money and send him on his way!"

"All right."

"And don't do anything else until you hear from me—and don't panic!"

The man nodded jerkily, and Clifton wondered how much longer he'd be able to bear up.

"All right, get out of here."

The man stood up and walked to the door. He turned

as if he were going to say something else, then thought better of it and left.

Clifton didn't know why he should help the man, except for the fact that he had helped set the other up in business years ago. Still, it was the other man who was in danger, and not he, so why should he get involved?

Let him solve his own problems, for once—and if the man hadn't been his brother-in-law, he would have.

There was a knock on the door, and he called out for whoever it was to come in.

"Gary?" Mona Wilcox entered the room. She was a tall willowy blonde who had been working for him for a couple of months.

"Hi, sweetheart. Come on in."

Mona closed the door and entered. Clifton got up and walked over to her. As he went to put his arms around her she backed away.

"What's wrong?"

"Your wife is outside."

"Barbara? What does she want?"

"Maybe she wants to know where you were all night."

"She knew about the game."

"Then why is she giving me dirty looks?"

Now he did put his arms around her and said, "She gives all the girls who work for me dirty looks, honey. She doesn't know anything."

He kissed her then, and she melted against him and kissed him back enthusiastically.

"All right," he said, "send her in."

"Wait."

She produced a handkerchief and cleaned her lipstick off his mouth.

"There."

"Thanks. Send her in. I'll get rid of her."

Mona went to the door and stepped outside where Clifton knew the bartender was keeping Barbara Clifton busy. Moments later Barbara burst into the room.

"You didn't come home last night!" she said.

Barbara Clifton was about thirty-five—ten years older than Mona—and she was a handsome woman. Her hair was chestnut-colored and rich, her eyes brown and large, with lines beginning to form at the corners. She was worried about those lines, and the more worried she got the more jealous she got.

"Honey, the game ran late," he said, moving to put his arms around her.

"Don't touch me!" she said, jumping back. "You smell like cheap perfume, like one of your saloon girls. Which one is it this time? That skinny blonde?"

"Honey, don't say that—"

"Don't sweet talk me, Gary. I came to talk to you about my brother."

"What about him?"

"Is he all right?"

"He's fine, as far as I can see. Why?"

"He doesn't seem right to me. He's been acting strangely."

"Well, he was just here and he seemed fine."

"I saw him leaving."

"Don't worry about him, Barbara. He's a big boy and can take care of himself."

"No, he can't. That's what the problem is."

"There *is* no problem, and even if there was, you know I'd take care of it."

"Sure, like you take care of everything and everybody else—except me."

"Come on, honey, don't—"

"I told you not to try that stuff on me—Oh, I don't even know why I bother. You were out all night, and I guess I just wanted to see if you were still alive."

"Well, I am," he said, spreading his hands. "Satisfied?"

She hesitated, then said, "No, somehow I don't think I am," and stormed out of the office.

Clifton sighed and sat behind his desk. After Clint Adams had left he had gone straight to Mona Wilcox's bed. As beautiful as Barbara had been when he married her, even then he hadn't been able to stay away from other women. Now that younger women were available—and willing—it was even more difficult.

And he didn't want to.

Barbara Clifton's brother returned to his store, where he often took refuge from the rest of the world. His days were often made up of going from his home to his store, and then back again. The only times he really got out were those three or four times a month that he played poker with Clifton, Leadbetter, and the others—and truth be told, he couldn't even afford to do that. He needed those men, however, as friends—or at least, he needed to think of them as his friends.

He'd always known that the day would come when someone who could identify him would come to town, but he hadn't expected it to be this man. Supposedly he had been taken care of the last time he was here— and now he was back, and with help.

And what help!

The Gunsmith.

Nervously the man went to the front window of his store and looked outside. He dreaded the possibility of the very man he feared coming into his store. What *could* he do then if not the very thing that Clifton had warned him not to do: panic!

He went back behind his counter, because that was where he kept his gun. If that sonofabitch did come into the store, even by accident, he was going to be met by a bullet.

SEVENTEEN

"How would you feel about being bait?" Clint asked.

He and Laramie were walking around the town, once again allowing Laramie to study the faces of the townspeople in an attempt to identify someone.

"Come again?"

"Bait. That stuff you put on the end of a fish hook and dangle in the—"

"I know what bait is, Clint. What do you mean, how would I feel about being bait? Isn't that what we are?"

"That's right," Clint said, "at the moment that's what we are, bait. I want to know how you would feel about taking the role on alone?"

"You've still got to explain this to me—slowly."

"It's simple. I leave town, and you don't. That leaves you on the end of the hook all by yourself."

"To do what?"

"To draw out the man from your dream."

"And where will you be?"

"Around."

"I get it. I walk around with a target on my forehead, and when he kills me, you grab him. Hey, nothing wrong with that plan that I can see."

"Except for one thing—you don't get killed. I grab him before he can kill you."

"You hope."

"Well, I would do my best," Clint said, contriving to sound hurt by Laramie's lack of confidence.

"Have you got any other bright ideas?"

"As a matter of fact, I do," Clint said. "What if we announce loudly in the saloon that we're leaving in the morning, and that we'll be traveling north."

"That would set us up as targets out there again. That didn't work so well last time."

"Maybe this time it will," Clint said, but Laramie wasn't listening. "What's wrong?"

Laramie looked at Clint and said, "That woman that just passed us. Did you notice her?"

"Of course I noticed her. Chestnut hair, full, womanly figure, handsome voice, big brown eyes—what about her?"

"There's something familiar about her."

"What?"

Laramie stopped and turned to watch the woman's

retreating back. She was walking along at a brisk pace, carrying some packages in her arms. She seemed to be hurrying to get where she was going before she dropped them—only she wasn't going to make it.

Clint, seeing that she was about to drop her burden, said, "Let's see if I can't find out something about her. See you back at the hotel."

Before Laramie could say anything Clint was rushing toward the woman, who was losing the package from the very top of her stack.

"Whoa there," Clint said, catching one before it hit the ground.

"Oh, thank you," she said, and suddenly the next one slid off, and Clint caught that one, too.

"Oh, God," she said.

"You look like you could use some help."

"Yes, I could, thank you," she said.

"Here," he said, setting the two packages back on top, "let me take the whole pile."

"Oh, no. . . ." She started to protest, but he lifted them easily from her.

"There. Now point me in the right direction and we're off."

"I really shouldn't—well, thank you. I live this way. At least let me take the top one."

"All right," he said, bending his knees so she could reach it. "This way," she said again.

"My name is Clint Adams."

"My name is Barbara, Mr. Adams—"

"Please, call me Clint. Have you been shopping for some sort of an occasion?"

"Oh, no, nothing special. Well," she said sheepishly, "actually, I had a fight with my husband, and when that happens I go shopping."

"A fight, eh? I can't see how any man married to you would have time to fight with you."

"I don't—" she began, frowning, obviously unsure about what he meant.

"I only meant that if I were married to a woman as beautiful as you I'd be too busy keeping her happy to fight with her."

Now she understood that it was a compliment, and she was pleased.

"Well, thank you. I only wish my husband felt the same way."

She led him to a large woodframe house that was set back off the main street. Since they had chatted all the way, now that they had arrived the moment seemed awkward.

"Well, here's where I live."

"I could put the packages down here—" he said, meaning the porch, but she interrupted him.

"Would you like to come in for some lemonade?"

"That would be nice," he said, "but your husband. . . ."

"My husband won't be home for quite some time," she said. "We had a fight, remember?"

He wondered if she was inviting him in because she was angry at her husband, but whatever the reason, he took advantage of it.

"All right, then. Let's have some lemonade."

"Good," she said smiling.

Once inside she showed him where to put the packages and invited him to wait in the living room. While she was in the kitchen he looked around, but found nothing to tell him who she might be.

When she came back bearing a tray with two glasses of lemonade he noticed that she had changed. There must have been another door from the kitchen to another part of the house, and she had gone to her bedroom and changed her dress. She had been wearing a high-necked dress which showed off her busty form, but now she was wearing a low-cut day dress which showed him the freckled upper slopes of her full breasts.

"Here's your lemonade," she said, bending over so he could reach the glass. He also got a long look down the front of her dress, and since it was obviously deliberate, he decided to comment on it.

She took her glass and sat next to him on the couch.

"Are those real?" he asked.

"What?" she asked, her eyes widening.

"Those," he said. Using his index finger he very delicately touched the upper slopes of her breasts. Her flesh was firm and smooth.

"The freckles, you mean?" she asked.

"Yes."

"Oh, yes, they're real," she said. "In fact, they go all the way . . . down," she added, sliding her finger down between her breasts.

"Do you have them anywhere else?"

"Umm," she said, as if deciding whether or not she should tell him, "actually, I've got them on my, uh, back and my, um, derriere. . . ."

"Really," he said, "how interesting. . . ."

"This is silly," she said, putting her glass down on the floor.

"What is?"

"These games," she said. "We've only just met and already we're playing word games. If you want to have sex with me, just say so."

He had been taking his first real good look at her. Her eyes were lovely, her mouth full and inviting. There were lines around her eyes and mouth, and he felt they might be not be lines of age so much as bitterness. She was very lovely.

"I'd be foolish to say anything but yes," he said, putting his glass on the table, "but in your present condition, I'd be less than a gentleman—"

"Fuck that," she said, and reached for him.

She came into his arms anxiously, her tongue blossoming in his mouth.

"As soon as I saw you on the street I knew this would happen," she said breathlessly.

"So did I," he lied.

EIGHTEEN

When she removed the dress he saw that she was telling the truth. The freckles went all the way down to the valley between her breasts and made a scattered pattern over the heavy, lower portions of her breasts. He cupped her breasts in his hands, hefting them, and she closed her eyes to his touch.

He turned her around and saw that she had freckles on her back and buttocks.

"Did you think I lied?"

"If anything," he said, "you weren't truthful enough."

She wrinkled her nose — which was curiously devoid of freckles — and said, "They're terrible, aren't they?"

"They're beautiful," he said.

"Well, let's see if you have any, then."

Clint was dubious about this, worried about what would happen if her husband came home, but the naked Barbara was even more enticing than the fully-clothed woman had been. She was sturdily built, with strong hips, thighs, and legs.

Finally he undressed.

"Well," she said, inspecting him, "no freckles, but I don't see anything else to complain about." To illustrate her point she closed her hand around his swollen penis and now it was he who closed his eyes as her other hand gently cupped his testicles.

She went down to her knees then and began to use her mouth on him. This was something that Clifton had taught her years ago, when they were first married. Oh, she knew then that he was much more experienced than she was, but she didn't care. She had thoroughly enjoyed learning everything he had to teach her, including all the different ways to satisfy a man, and she had learned quite well.

As for Clifton, that sonofabitch had probably forgotten how good she was, it had been that long since they'd been together.

She needed this, she thought, sucking on Clint Adams' rigid penis. She needed this very badly, and she was going to enjoy it—and so was Clint.

She needn't have worried about Clint Adams, though. He was enjoying himself thoroughly, at the moment, cupping her head in his hand as she bobbed up and down on the length of him, wetting him, suckling him, building him to a point of peak readiness—and then abandoning him.

"Oh, so you're a tease, eh?" he asked as she moved away from him.

"I'm not a tease," she said breathlessly, "I'm ready." She turned around and with her hands on the couch bent all the way over, presenting him with the smooth, round moons of her generous rear end. She spread her legs and said, "I'm not teasing, Clint, I'm just ready."

He moved in behind her and was able to smell her readiness. He put a hand on either hip, poked his penis between her thighs, found the moist portal of her sex and thrust himself in.

Over the years Clint had taken women many different ways, and although most of them had preferred it face to face, he had found some who preferred to take a man this way. In some cases, he had found that he was able to achieve an incredible depth of penetration in this position, and Barbara—he hadn't even gotten her last name—seemed to be one of these cases.

He seemed to penetrate right to the very core of her and she began to ride him, moving back and forth on him, gasping and grunting with the effort.

"Oh, yes," she said, "Oh, my, yes . . . oh Clint, harder, do it harder . . ."

Soon he was able to match her tempo, so that when she moved back he moved forward, and the air was filled with the noise of their flesh slapping together. First it went slap . . . slap . . . slap . . . slap . . .

And then *slap-slap-slap-slap* as their ardor increased. . . .

And finally slapslapslapslap . . . and Clint groaned as he began to fill her, and she cried out as she began to climax, burying her face in the cushions of the couch . . .

It was only moments later when they coupled again in a more conventional manner, after she had used her mouth again to bring him to readiness.

This time they fell together onto the couch with Clint on top, and as he pierced her she gasped and wrapped her powerful legs around him. He slid his hands beneath her to grasp her and hold her close, and he knew that he'd be in deep shit if the door should open and her husband should walk in, but even that thought did not dampen his need for her, a need that was fueled by her obvious and desperate need for him.

She moaned and cried out and scratched him as he fucked her, and when she came she bit his shoulder, then screamed against him when he exploded inside of her . . . .

As he dressed she lay on the couch, still naked, her legs wide open, her breasts flattening and falling to the sides slightly, victims of their own voluptuousness, not an unpleasant sight at all. She was watching him and idly twirling her public hair around her finger.

"You know," she said, dreamily, "I don't think I've ever felt this sexy, this sensuous before." She stretched, pulling her breasts taut and then relaxing again, and he was tempted to undress again, but that would have been pushing his—and her—luck.

He strapped on his gun and said, "You'd better get dressed."

"Why? Do you think my husband hasn't seen me naked, before? Well, you're right. He hasn't, not lately. He's too busy fucking the girls that work for him, the younger girls that he hires."

"Then he's a fool," Clint said, "he doesn't know what he has."

"No, he doesn't, does he?"

"Maybe you should tell him."

She made a face.

"I've been trying to tell him, but he isn't listening to me. He's too wrapped up in his business, in this town, and in his romances."

"Is he a prominent man in town?" Clint asked. "I don't even know your last name."

"Oh, he's prominent, all right," she said, but just as she seemed ready to reveal his name something occurred to her, and she sat up. "When are you leaving town, Clint?"

"I don't know, really. Maybe in a couple of days."

"I'll have to see you again before you leave, of course. At least one more time. Can we do that?"

"Barbara, I really don't like interfering in a marriage—"

"But you're not. My marriage was interfered with long before you. Please Clint, just one more time. I really need it and . . . and no man has ever made me feel . . . this way."

"What way?"

"Wanted . . . sexy . . . beautiful. . . ."

"But you are all of those things," he said. He went to her and she put her arms around his neck, staying seated as they kissed. He reached between them and fondled her breasts, tweaking the nipples.

"God," she said against his mouth, "you make me shameless."

He kissed her shortly and straightened up.

"I do insist on one thing, though."

"What's that?"

"Knowing who you are."

She smiled and said, "I thought you were going to ask for something hard, like wanting me to stay quiet the next time you slide that beautiful tool of yours between my legs. My name's Clifton, Barbara Clifton."

"Clifton?" he said. "You're married to Gary Clifton, the man who owns the saloon?"

"The same," she said. "Do you know my husband?"

"I know him," he said. "I don't like him, but I know him."

"Well," she said, grinning, "that's one more thing we've got in common."

NINETEEN

Clint found Laramie waiting for him in front of the hotel. He was sitting in a straightbacked wooden chair, his feet pressed against a post.

"How'd it go?" Laramie asked.

"In some ways better than others," Clint said, sitting on the steps.

"What's that mean?"

"That woman is Gary Clifton's wife."

"The saloon owner?"

"Yep."

"Did you find out anything from her?"

"Yeah," Clint said. "She's lonely."

"How lonely?"

"Let's just say that if her husband had walked in on us he wouldn't have been pleased."

"That lonely, huh?"

"Yeah," Clint said, not feeling very proud of himself at the moment. He liked the woman, but the liaison was a dangerous one, and he knew that he shouldn't see her any more.

"What have you been doing?" he asked Laramie.

"I've been sitting here watching faces."

"Any familiar ones?"

"No." Laramie frowned and said, "What I still can't figure out is why that woman's face. . . . "

"Barbara Clifton's?"

"Right. Why this Barbara Clifton's face seemed familiar."

"Maybe she looks like someone you knew in your past. A girlfriend. A—" Clint stopped short, but Laramie had already caught on.

"A wife?" he asked. "A wife who's wondering why the hell her husband didn't come back to her? And maybe some kids, as well?"

"Laramie—"

"I know, I know. When I start thinking like that I get depressed."

They sat in silence for a while, and then Laramie said, "I've been thinking about what you said."

"Which time?"

"About me playing bait."

"And?"

"I think it's the only way."

"We can talk about it."

"No, let's not talk about it," Laramie said, "let's do it."

"All right," Clint said, "let's compromise."

"How?"

Clint looked at Laramie and said, "Let's talk about it now."

Later they entered the Laramie Saloon and saw Gary Clifton. He waved a hand at Clint and walked over.

"Well?" Clint asked.

"Nothing," Laramie said.

When Clifton reached them he put his hand out and shook hands with Clint.

"I'm glad you came by, Clint. And this is your friend?"

"Yes. Laramie Jones, this is Gary Clifton."

"Well, Laramie," Clifton said, shaking hands, "how interesting. Is this a coincidence?"

"Not exactly. I always wanted to see the town I was named after."

"And what do you think of it?"

"I've found it a little less than friendly."

"Yes, yes, I've heard about your unfortunate incidents. In fact, everyone in town has heard about them."

"It's enough to make you leave town," Clint said.

"Not me," Laramie said, and the tone of his voice caused Clifton to look closely at both men.

"Why don't we sit down and have a drink?" Clifton suggested.

"Good idea," Clint said.

The place was crowded, but there was a table in the back that was empty. Clint assumed it was Clifton's table, and was therefore always available for him.

They sat and he waved his arm, bringing a pretty blond girl over to their table.

"Beer, gentlemen? Or something stronger?"

"Beer's fine," Clint said, and Laramie nodded.

"Mona, bring three beers, please."

"Right away, boss."

Mona walked to the bar, and while Clifton watched Mona, Clint watched Clifton. He believed some of the things Barbara had told him, now that he had seen the man undress one of his girls with his eyes.

Mona returned and leaned over to put some beer down. She was tall and willowy, but with firm, round breasts. She gave her boss a special smile and Clint and Laramie a less special one before leaving.

"Nice-looking girl," Clint commented.

"Hmm. Oh, yes. I try to employ the prettiest girls I can find."

"That one certainly fills the bill," Laramie said, still watching her.

"What do they do besides serve drinks?" Clint asked.

"That's between them and the customers, Clint. All I pay them to do is serve drinks and mingle."

"Nice arrangement."

Laramie sat and brooded into his beer.

"Excuse me, my friend," Clifton said to him, "but you look as if you have something serious on your mind. Is there anything I can help you with?"

"You can talk my friend here out of leaving town," Laramie said.

"Laramie," Clint said warningly, "that's between you and me."

"Are you leaving so soon?" Clifton asked Clint.

"Yeah," Clint said after a moment, "I'm a little tired of getting shot at."

"I would have thought you'd be used to that by now, what with your reputation, and all."

"With my reputation and all," Clint said slowly, "I'm a little tired of getting shot at."

"I told you they were shooting at me, not you," Laramie said.

"Well, the bullets came just as close to me as they did to you," Clint said. "I'd say it was a toss-up."

"Why would they be shooting at you?" Clifton asked Laramie.

Laramie opened his mouth to answer, then closed it as if he thought better of it.

"I just have a feeling, is all."

"Well, will you be leaving town with Clint?"

"No. I'm staying."

"You have business here?"

"You could say that."

"Damned fool, if you ask me," Clint said. "Any town where they shoot at you for blinking is no town to stay in, believe me."

"I'm staying."

"So stay! Get killed while you're at it."

"Maybe you two fellows will excuse me," Clifton said, rising. "You seem to have some unfinished business. I'll leave you alone to settle it."

Clifton left the table, watched carefully by Clint and Laramie as he crossed the room and entered his office.

"Think he went for it?" Laramie asked.

"I'm sure of it."

"What if you're wrong about him?"

"I don't think I am," Clint said thoughtfully. "My guess is still that whoever is shooting at you has a position to protect here, otherwise why go to such drastic measures? If he does have a position, then he's got to have some connection with Clifton, another man with a position in town. Besides, Clifton is just too damned eager to be of service to a couple of strangers."

"And what if it's Clifton himself?"

"Then the message has already been delivered, hasn't it?"

"I guess so."

A little while later the blond, Mona, came over with two more beers.

"Compliments of the house," she said, smiling brightly.

"Thank you, Mona," Clint said.

"You're welcome."

"Uh, Mona," Clint said as she was turning away.

"Yes, sir."

"Mr. Clifton didn't leave, did he?"

"Uh, no sir. I don't think so. He's in his office."

"Isn't there another way out of his office?"

"Yes sir, another door leading to the back, but he

usually doesn't leave during business."

"All right. Thank you."

"You're welcome."

After she left Laramie followed her with his eyes and then said, "You think he left already to deliver the message?"

"That's my guess," Clint said. "He's probably talking to whoever shot at us right now."

TWENTY

Clifton had gone into his office, crossed the room, and left by the back way. He went to his brother-in-law's house and banged on the door until he answered.

"What the hell—" the man said, opening the door. He stopped when he saw who it was.

"Let me in."

"What's wrong?"

"Nothing," Clifton said, entering and closing the door behind him. "I just got some news for you."

"If it's bad, I don't want to hear it."

"Clint Adams is pulling out."

"So? He's not the one I'm worried about."

"He's the one you should be worried about. As long

111

as he's around, this Laramie Jones has got as much chance of getting you as you have of getting him. Without Adams to back him up, he won't be hard to take care of at all."

"You sayin' what I think you're sayin'?"

"Yes, I am. Once the Gunsmith is gone, we'll take care of Mr. Laramie Jones."

"Who's gonna do it?"

"Don't worry about that. I'll get somebody who won't miss."

Clifton opened the door to leave, then couldn't resist turning to his brother-in-law and saying, "If it wasn't for Barbara, I'd let you solve your own problems."

"I appreciate it, Gary. Really I do."

"Yeah, sure. Go to sleep. You're safe for tonight."

Clifton left, and the other man leaned on the door and heaved a sigh of relief. Maybe by tomorrow night this would all be over with.

When Clifton came out of his office, Clint was sure that he had just come in from outside. It was the look of him that gave it away. Mona went over to him and said something and then he walked over to their table.

"Well, my friends, have you settled your differences?" he asked.

"Yes," Clint said. "I'll be leaving in the morning, so I'd better get some sleep."

"That's a shame," Clifton said. "We could have had some interesting conversations."

"Maybe another time," Clint said. He looked at Laramie, as if he wanted to say something, then simply shook his head and left.

"And you?" Clifton asked.

Laramie looked at him and said, "I'm always ready for some interesting conversation."

"Oh, I'm sorry. Perhaps another time?" Clifton said. "I have some business to attend to."

"Yeah," Laramie said to himself as Clifton walked away. "So do I."

In his room Clint became convinced that they had missed a perfect opportunity. He hadn't needed Laramie in the saloon. He could have convinced Clifton himself that he was leaving and Laramie was staying, and then Laramie could have followed Clifton when he left the saloon.

Stupid, he thought. Like having sex with Clifton's wife. Just plain stupid.

Clint lay on the bed and thought, Jesus, I must be getting old.

Laramie got drunk.

That wasn't his first mistake. His first mistake was staying at the saloon after Clint left. He should have left and went to the second whorehouse, but the funny thing was he had taken a liking to Mona. He enjoyed watching her walk around the room, serving drinks, dodging drunks with fast—and not so fast—hands. And he liked the way she leaned over him when she served him his beer.

"What do you do after this place closes?" he asked.

"What do I do? I go home."

"Where's home?"

"Why?"

"I want to walk you there."

"I have a room upstairs."

"Here?"

"Yes, here."

"Convenient."

"What does that mean?"

"Nothing. I'm sorry. Can I come up?"

"No."

"Why not?"

"We lock up after we close."

"So?"

"I can't keep anyone in here."

"Then come back to my hotel with me."

"No."

"Why not? I'll pay you."

"That doesn't matter."

"Hey," he said, reaching for her arm.

"I'm sorry," she said, pulling away.

She went to the bar, where Clifton came over to her.

"What did he want?"

"Me."

"For the night?"

"Yes, at his hotel."

Clifton looked at Laramie, whose head was almost in his beer mug, and said, "Go with him."

"Why?"

"Because I want you to," Clifton said. "What's wrong? Isn't he good-looking enough?"

"He's good-looking. . . ."

"So?"

"Why, Gary?"

"Because I want to know where he is tonight, and where he'll be tomorrow. Come back here in the morning and let me know."

She glared at him and he thought, this is what happens when you sleep with the stock. If he was a rancher, he wouldn't sleep with one of the cows, would he? Maybe he should just save that stuff for Barbara.

"All right," she said. "All right."

"Charge him a lot. He'll pay."

"You bet I will."

She walked over to Laramie's table and said, "I've changed my mind."

He looked up at her bleary-eyed and said, "Really? When can you leave?"

"Now," she said, reaching for his arm, "right now."

TWENTY-ONE

The knock at the door surprised Clint. He moved to the door and asked, "Who is it?"

The answer surprised him even more than the knock itself had.

"Susan Bell."

"One moment."

He hastily pulled on his pants, then decided to leave the shirt off and go barechested. What did she expect for a surprise visit, fancy dress?

He opened the door and said, "Come in."

She was still wearing trail clothes, but as she passed him to enter, her scent was unmistakably feminine, no matter how mannish her clothes were.

"It's a little late for visiting, isn't it?"

When she turned around, he noticed something else about her. She had been drinking.

"I suppose so," she said. "And I suppose I should apologize—but I'm not."

"There's no need to. Why don't you sit down?"

"Thank you," she said, and promptly sat down on his bed.

"I'm sorry I don't have anything to offer you."

"That's all right," she said, "I have my own." She produced a hip flask and offered it to him. He took it out of curiosity and found that it was filled with very good brandy.

"That's very good."

"You know good liquor when you taste it, eh?"

"Some."

She tilted the flask back and he watched her smooth throat work as she drank. When she put the flask back in her pocket, he saw that her eyes were glassy. She wouldn't last much longer.

"Can we get to the point of this visit *before* you pass out?" he asked.

"Pass out?" she asked. Standing up very quickly she said, "Are you under the impression that I cannot hold my . . . my—"

He moved quickly, but not quickly enough to catch her. Luckily when she fell, she did so in the direction of the bed. The springs squeaked as she landed, and he stared at her.

What was he supposed to do with her now?

• • •

What was she supposed to do with him now, Mona wondered.

She stood next to the bed, naked, staring down at the sleeping figure of Laramie Jones—who actually was not sleeping, but had passed out. How could she get any information out of him now—and more to the point, why should she even have tried? Obviously, she'd been wrong about Gary Clifton. She thought he cared for her, but no man who cared for a woman would ask her to sleep with another man.

So she was glad Jones had passed out. Maybe she should just get dressed and go back to the saloon, only it would be locked up by now and she'd have to bang on the door to be let in. Once inside, she'd have to explain to Clifton what had happened, and she didn't feel like talking to him now. She decided she'd sleep here.

If Laramie Jones would stop snoring, that is.

Clint had never heard a woman snore the way Susan Bell did. He'd never be able to get to sleep. He decided to go down the hall to Laramie's room to see if he could use his floor for the night.

He lifted Susan Bell's legs up onto the bed, removed her boots, and covered her with the bedclothes, then went down the hall barefoot, clad only in pants, and knocked on Laramie's door.

The knock came as a surprise to Mona. What was she supposed to do, answer it or ignore it? What if it was Clifton? No, why would he come? To stop her from sleeping with Laramie Jones?

Sure.

"Who is it?" she asked.

There was a long pause, and then a voice said, "Clint Adams."

That was the man who had been sitting with Laramie Jones at the saloon. Now there was an interesting-looking man. If Clifton had asked her to sleep with him. . . .

She put on one of Laramie's shirts to cover her nakedness, unlocked the door and opened it.

"Oh, hi," he said.

"Hi."

"I didn't mean to interrupt."

"You're not," she said, giving him an ironic look. She stepped aside so he could see Laramie on the bed.

"Passed out?"

"Cold."

"We seem to have a similar problem," he said.

"Really?"

He explained to her what had happened, and then added, "And mine is snoring, too."

Boldly, she said, "I have an idea."

"I'm game."

She explained it to him, and Clint liked it.

"After all," she said by way of explanation, "I have nowhere else to go."

Neither of them had come up with the idea of renting another room—or if they had, they had each dismissed it.

"Who do we move?" she asked. "Him or her?"

"Her," Clint said. "You can get the doors, and I can carry her."

"All right."

They set about making the exchange. Both were still seminaked as they went down the hall to Clint's room. Inside, he picked up the soundly sleeping Susan Bell, carried her down the hall and into Laramie's room, where he deposited her on the bed next to Laramie. There they lay, side by side, blissfully snoring.

"Bring your things," Clint told Mona.

She gathered up her clothing and, still wearing Laramie's shirt, followed Clint down the hall to his room.

"Well," he said, "at least now we'll be able to get some sleep."

"If we want to," she said.

He turned in time to see Laramie's shirt fall from her shoulders to the floor. He didn't show surprise, because he thought they had both made this decision as soon as she opened Laramie's door.

After all, she *was* extremely pretty

TWENTY-TWO

Mona woke Clint the next morning, running her tongue over his flaccid penis. Immediately even before he was even fully awake, she had him hard.

"Good morning," she said, peering up at him from over his swollen penis.

"Good morning. Did you sleep well?"

"Wonderful," she said. "And you?"

"Fine."

"Are you well-rested enough?"

"For what?"

"Silly man," she said, and took him into her lovely, talented mouth.

• • •

In the other room, Susan Bell stirred, a band of sunlight from the window falling across her eyes. She picked her arm up to cover her eyes, and realized that she wasn't wearing her nightgown. In fact, she was dressed.

"What the—" she said, sitting up, and that was when she saw the man lying next to her.

She looked around in confusion, trying to determine where she was, and then looked at the sleeping man again. It took a moment, but she recognized him. The man who had been with Clint Adams when they'd first met.

Wait a minute, she thought. Last night she had left her ranch to come to the hotel to talk to Clint Adams again about taking a job. Sure, and she had also hoped to fall into his bed. She admitted that. It had been a long time since she'd seen a man she wanted, but she'd wanted him, almost from that first encounter.

Had she really gotten the wrong room and the wrong man?

Had she been that drunk?

She'd been drinking more and more lately, but this scared her. She couldn't remember what had happened last night. She didn't even remember if she and this man had. . . . But no. They were still both dressed, and he looked for all the world like someone passed out, not sleeping.

She swung her legs to the floor and stood up, experiencing just a short moment of vertigo. She had to get out of here and back to the ranch, where she could try and figure out what had happened.

She went to the door, opened it soundlessly, and slipped out.

Clint flipped Mona over and started to work on her breasts.

"For a skinny girl," he'd told her the night before, "you've got a pair of big, lovely breasts."

"They are my best feature," she had admitted.

"Oh, you have a lot of good features, Mona."

"Really?"

"Really," he'd told her, "and I intend to work on every one of them."

So now he was working on her breasts while she reached between their bodies, groping for his penis. He slipped away from her and traced a wet path down over her belly with his tongue.

"Oh lordy," she said, realizing what he was going to do. He had done it to her once during the night, and she had almost lost control. He was so *good* at it!

"Oh, yes . . . yes . . ." she moaned as he lapped at her. Even the slurping noses he made every so often excited her. When he slid his hands beneath her to cup her buttocks, she got that helpless feeling again, as if she were totally in his hands, in his power.

Then his tongue poked into her and she lifted her hips, reaching for his head, and then she was coming . . . Lordy, she was coming. . . .

When Laramie woke up, he licked his lips in an effort to wet them, but his tongue was just as dry as they were. He turned his head with some effort, and although he was alone on the bed, he saw the depression of another person in the pillow and mattress. For the life of him, though, he couldn't remember who that person might have been. The next thing he realized was that he was totally dressed.

He tried to lift his head, but failed.

Fuck it.

He was just too tired to try and figure it out now. He went back to sleep.

Mona was sitting astride Clint, the full length of him tucked neatly inside of her. She was leaning over him, her breasts dangling in his face, her hands pinning his to the bed above his head.

"I wonder . . . " she said.

He stopped sucking on her nipples for a moment and said, "You wonder what?"

"I wonder what your friends thought when they woke up and saw each other."

"One of them is my friend," he said, running his tongue around her right nipple, "the other is just an acquaintance."

"You mean you've never been to bed with that woman?" she asked.

"Never."

"Why did she come to your room last night?"

"I don't know," he said, circling the left nipple now. She had the smoothest skin, like warm marble. "I'll have to ask her—if she remembers, herself."

"Maybe she came to your room for the same reason I did," she suggested playfully.

"To get some sleep?"

She slapped him in the face with her breasts.

"No, love," she said, "for this." She clenched and unclenched her muscles, sucking on the length of him with her insides. He'd always marveled at women who had the ability to do that. He wondered if they practiced.

"If she did come for this," she said, lowering her head so that she could outline his mouth with her tongue, "I feel sorry for her—and glad for me."

"Let's stop talking about other people," he suggested.

She smiled and said, "Let's just stop talking . . . period."

"Deal."

TWENTY-THREE

"You look like you had a hard night," Clint said to
Laramie at breakfast.

"Don't remind me."

"I thought you'd come back with company."

"I did."

"Oh? Who?"

Looking embarrassed, Laramie said, "I can't remember."

"That must have been some night."

"I drank too much."

"You're kidding."

"Clint . . . could we talk about something else?"

"Sure," Clint said. "Let's talk about the odds of
one of us getting killed today. . . .

•   •   •

Mona returned to the saloon that morning, after leaving Clint's room early. She felt like a different woman, now that she knew that Gary Clifton was not the man for her. She should have realized that when she found out he was married, but it took finding a real man like Clint Adams to truly bring it home to her.

Of course, Clint *could* be the man for her, but she knew that he never *would* be. That was the difference between a Clint Adams and a Gary Clifton. With Clint she knew just where she stood—or where she lay—and that was fine with her.

"Mona, tell me the truth, now," Clint had said that morning.

"About what?" she'd asked, even though she knew what he was going to ask.

"Why did you come back to the hotel with Laramie?"

"Because Clifton told me to," she told him, without the slightest hesitation.

Clint had been surprised at her frankness.

"I can tell you that now, because . . . because of what happened between us."

"What happened between us was nice, Mona, but it can't be anything more than that."

"I know that."

"And you still want to tell me the truth?"

"Yes."

She'd then told him that Clifton wanted to know what Laramie's plans were, as well as Clint's.

"And he thought Laramie would talk to you in bed, while he was drunk and in the throes of passion."

"It's been known to happen," she'd said.

"Oh, yes, I know that. What are you going to tell Clifton?"

"I don't know."

"What if I tell you what to tell him? Would you?"

"What do you want me to say?" she'd asked, and then she'd listened intently while he told her what he wanted her to say.

"Can you do that for me?"

"Yes."

"You don't want to think about it?"

"What is there to think about? All that's necessary is for me to lie to a man. I've done that before, Clint. Haven't all women?"

"You seem to have a low opinion of women, Mona. I find that odd."

"Don't. I have a low opinion of people in general."

"I hope I haven't done anything to reinforce that opinion."

"Nothing at all," she'd said. "On the contrary, you're probably one of the nicest people I've ever met."

"I appreciate that, but—"

"Yes, I know. No promises. I'm not naive, Clint. At least," she'd said, recalling the way Gary Clifton had fooled her, "not anymore."

"Well, I've got one more thing to ask of you. Hopefully that won't change your opinion of me."

"It would have to be pretty bad to do that," she'd assured him. "What is it?"

He'd told her, and she'd agreed.

Now she knocked on the door of the saloon and

Pete, the bartender, opened up for her. Clifton was already there, having breakfast.

"Last night was unusual," Barbara Clifton told her husband that morning.

"Why?"

"You came home."

He was dressing, and she watched him totally without interest. He had slept of the couch, as he had been doing for the past week or so. She was glad that although he had come home early he hadn't tried to get into bed with her. After her session with Clint Adams, she didn't think she would have been able to stand that.

"I live here, Barbara," he said.

"Oh. You remember that, huh?"

He finished dressing and turned to face her.

"Things are going to be different from now on, Barbara," he said.

"Oh? Why is that?"

"Because I realized what a fool I've been. I've taken you for granted, and I'm going to make it up to you."

"How?"

"We'll have to talk about that."

"Sure," she said. "We'll talk."

He nodded, and then left the house. She went to the front window to watch him walk away, thinking: Too little too late, buddy.

When Mona walked in, Clifton looked at her and thought about how beautiful she was. Then he remembered the promise he'd made to Barbara that morning.

Oh, well, it certainly wouldn't be the first promise he'd broken.

"Good morning, Mona," he said. "Have some coffee?"

"Sure," she said, sitting opposite him.

"How was your night?"

She made a face before answering. Clint had told her to be sure she did that.

"It was all right."

He laughed.

"Yes, I can see by the look on your face. I'm sorry I had to make you go through that, but I'm going to make it up to you. I promise."

"That's all right."

"What did our young friend tell you?"

"Just what they told you last night," she said. "Adams is leaving this morning, and Laramie is staying. He said he's here to find someone."

"Really? He didn't tell me that last night."

"Well, then," she said, "maybe I did some good last night."

"I'm sure you did," Clifton said. "I'm sure you were very good last night."

"So, how are we going to work this?" Laramie asked after breakfast.

"I'm going to saddle up and ride out and then double back. You'll have to give me enough time to do that, and then start walking around town again."

"There's no guarantee that he'll try for me again in town," Laramie said. "And besides, we've walked all over town already, and I haven't seen anyone familiar.''

"That's right, we've walked all over town, but what haven't we done?''

Laramie frowned and asked, "What?''

"We haven't gone into all of the stores, Laramie. If our man is man of position, he must own some sort of business in town.''

"That makes sense,'' Laramie said. "So I start going into stores. . . .''

"And if he gets nervous again, he'll make another try at you.''

"And you'll be there to stop him.''

"Right.''

"After you've doubled back.''

"Right.''

"What happens if you don't double back? What happens if he takes you out first?''

"He won't.''

"How do you know that?''

"I won't let him.''

Laramie gave Clint a stern look.

"Look, Laramie, I'll be real careful and watch my back. I promise.''

"How will I know if you're there or not?''

"Well, I can't come to see you. In fact, you might not even recognize me.,''

"What are you going to do, change your face?''

Clint smiled, thinking of his arrangement with Mona.

"That's exactly what I'm going to do.''

TWENTY-FOUR

After Clint left Laramie, he went directly to the livery stable to saddle his horse.

"Leaving already?" the liveryman asked.

"I've had just about enough of Laramie, thank you."

"I've never had a horse like that in my stable," the man said. "It's a pleasure just knowing he's there."

"Thanks," Clint said, paying the man and giving him something extra for taking good care of Duke.

The man surprised him by giving it back.

"It was my pleasure, Mr. Adams."

"Thank you."

Clint mounted up and rode out of town. True to his word, he was extra careful about watching his back trail, not wanting another ambush like the other day.

He rode in a circle around Laramie, in order to be quite sure he wasn't being followed. Apparently his plan had paid off. Whoever the man was, he was content with letting Clint Adams ride out of town, presumably sure that he was through with him.

Now the man could concentrate on his real target.

Satisfied that he wasn't being followed, Clint changed his course and headed for his meeting with Mona.

Gary Clifton went to see his brother-in-law in his store just as he opened.

"What's wrong?" the man asked.

"Nothing," Clifton said. "Nothing at all. I just wanted to tell you that the Gunsmith is gone. He rode out of town this morning."

The brother-in-law heaved a sigh of relief.

"Now we can take care of Laramie Jones."

"You just sit tight," Clifton said. "I've already got that covered."

As Clifton left, his brother-in-law was so happy, he almost forgot how much he hated the bastard for the way he treated him and his sister.

Clint had a friend in the United States Secret Service who was an expert at disguises, and Clint had learned a thing or two from him. His friend taught him that you could change your appearance with very little difficulty. A change of clothing and a new way of walking—shuffling your feet, hunching your shoulders—went a long way toward changing the way you appeared to people. The addition of some fake facial hair would simply make the change that much more effective.

Mona was waiting for Clint at the prearranged place just north of town.

"You're on time," she said.

"Good," he said, dismounting. "I hoped you weren't waiting long. Did you get everything?"

"I did," she said, indicating the bundle on the ground. "What do you intend to do with all this stuff?"

"Change the way I look."

"So you can go back into town?"

"That's right."

"Why not just leave?"

"My friend's in town, and he's counting on me to back him up. I'm standing between him and dying."

"He must trust you very much."

"I hope he does. You'd better go back to town now, Mona. Clifton may be wondering where you've gone."

"He gave me some money for doing a good job," she said. "I told him I was going to buy a new dress."

"Then you'd better buy one," he said, "so he doesn't get suspicious."

"I already have. I have to pick it up later."

Clint went to her and kissed her. He meant it to be a brief kiss of thanks, but she clung to him until they were both breathless.

"Not here," he said.

"I know," she said. "I hope everything goes well for you, Clint, but I hope you won't leave until I can . . . see you again."

"I'll see you again," he said. "Don't worry."

She nodded, then mounted her mare with his help. She looked down at him and said, "Good luck."

"Thanks," he said as she rode away, "I'm going to need it."

There was something Clint had not considered.

Once he was properly disguised—different clothes, a fake mustache and new walk—he realized that he had not taken Duke into consideration. If he rode into town on the big black gelding, his disguise would be useless. He couldn't very well leave Duke out here indefinitely, though. He considered riding to Susan Bell's ranch and asking for her help, but after the way he'd turned down her offer of the job, he wasn't so sure he'd get it. Besides, he had little time to waste before Laramie started hitting the stores and shops in town.

He finally decided to walk the big gelding into town and try to get to the livery without being seen. Then he'd have to slip the liveryman something extra—and make him take it, this time—to keep Duke out of sight.

With that problem solved, he thought his plan was ready to put in effect, and maybe it might even work.

TWENTY-FIVE

Actually, it didn't take long for the plan to work. Clint was pleasantly surprised.

He took to the rooftops as soon as he returned to town, and it figured that anyone who was going to take a shot at Laramie would do the same. He shouldn't have been surprised, then, to find himself a rooftop away from the would-be killer, who was following Laramie, waiting for a clear shot.

All Clint had to do was make up that rooftop difference before the man took his shot. He could have shot the man from where he was, but they wanted him alive so he could talk.

Clint moved forward, hoping that the man would be too intent on Laramie to notice him before it was too late.

• • •

He was in a panic, which was just what Clifton had warned him against, but there he was, the man who could ruin everything for him, and he was about to enter his store. Briefly he considered running to the door and locking it, putting up his "Closed" sign, but then he decided against it.

He stood behind the counter, his hand on the gun underneath. If the man walked in, he would shoot him where he stood and claim he thought he was being robbed. That would work.

It would have to.

Laramie was tired.

He'd been going in and out of stores for almost two hours, and he had a cramp between his shoulders from keeping them hunched, waiting for a bullet. He had no way of knowing if Clint was around or not, and even though he trusted Clint, he couldn't seem to relax his shoulders.

He crossed the street, heading for the hardware store, unaware that death wasn't only waiting behind him, but in front of him, as well.

The man on the roof sighted down on Laramie Jones's back and began to mentally count his money. What he hadn't counted on was the cold steel that poked its way into his right ear.

"Put the rifle up, friend," Clint Adams said. "We've got some talking to do."

Laramie was about to enter the hardware store when

he heard the shot from behind him. Immediately he fell into a crouch, but when he looked up at the rooftops he saw that Clint Adams had fired the shot, and was now waving at him. Laramie stood up, waved back, and crossed the street again.

Inside the hardware store the man heard the shot and saw Laramie Jones crouch. Moments later, Jones was crossing the street away from his shop.

He didn't know what had happened, but he breathed a sigh of relief.

Laramie met Clint on the street, with his prisoner in tow.

"Who is he?" Laramie asked. "I don't recognize him."

"You wouldn't," Clint said. "He's just hired help, but he's going to tell us who he works for."

"Like hell I will," the man said. "You can turn me over to the sheriff and I won't talk."

"I don't have any intention of turning you over to the sheriff, friend," Clint said, "and you will talk."

The man gave Clint a puzzled look.

"We'll take him to the livery stable and question him there," Clint said. "Let's move fast before the sheriff comes to see what the shot was about."

As they pushed the man in the direction of the livery stable, Laramie looked at Clint and said, "You look like shit."

Clint pulled the phony mustache off his face and said, "You should talk, friend."

"Yeah," Laramie said, "but I always look this way."

TWENTY-SIX

It was a simple matter of progression from that point on. Once the gunman realized why Clint and Laramie had no intention of turning him over to the sheriff, he decided that it was better to talk right away than to undergo pain first.

"You've got to turn me over to the law," the man insisted as Clint and Laramie pushed him into the livery stable.

"No, we don't, friend," Clint said. "We prefer to take care of you ourselves. After all, we're the ones you've been shooting at."

"I ain't shot at neither of you!"

"What were you about to do to my friend here?" Clint asked.

"That's different, but up to now I ain't even laid eyes on either one of you. I was just hired yesterday."

"By who?"

The man opened his mouth to reply, then thought better of it.

"I can't tell you that."

"Sure you can," Clint said, "and you will. In there, please," Clint said, and shoved the man into an empty stall. The stall had an inordinate amount of hay in it, and the man stumbled and fell into it.

"Now just sit there and think about the question again," Clint said. "Who hired you?"

"I can't—what's that?" the man stammered.

"This?" Clint asked, holding up a lucifer match. "This is a match."

"And that's hay you're sitting in," Laramie pointed out.

"When I light the match and drop it into the hay," Clint explained, "the hay will burn."

"And when the hay burns," Laramie said, taking up the explanation, "so will you."

"You can't do that!"

"Yes," Clint said, striking the match to life, "we can."

"Now," Laramie said, "who hired you?"

The man couldn't take his eyes off the match as it burned down toward Clint's thumb.

"I'm not letting my finger get burned, friend," Clint said. "I'll drop it into the hay first."

"You wouldn't—"

"Whoops!" Clint said, dropping the match.

"All right! All right! It was Clifton, Gary Clifton,

the guy who owns the saloon. Jesus, put it out!"

It took the three of them, but they did finally put the fire out.

"Sheriff?" Clint called out after the main fire had been stamped out. "Did you get all of that?"

"I did, Adams," the sheriff said, stepping out of an empty stall.

"Why don't you put this nice cooperative gentleman in your jail while we go over and have a talk with the man who hired him: Mr. Gary Clifton."

"I'll do just that."

"We'll meet you over there," Clint said.

"You took a big chance with that fire, Adams," the lawman said.

"Would you take a chance of burning for somebody else?"

"No, not me."

"Nobody would," Clint assured him. "Come on, Laramie. Let's find out why Clifton wants you dead."

"He's not here," the bartender said.

"Where is he, then?" Clint asked.

The bartender shrugged.

"Look, friend—"

"Clint."

Clint turned and saw Mona coming down the stairs. "What is it?" she asked.

"Clifton's the man we're looking for, Mona."

"He went home, Clint. He said he'd be back later."

"Stay here," he told her. "Send the sheriff over when he arrives." To Laramie he said, "Come on."

• • •

Barbara Clifton answered the door and gasped when she saw Clint.

"Not now," she said, urgently. "My husband is home."

"I know," Clint said. "I came to see him."

"Are you going to ask for my hand?" she asked, laughing.

"No," Clint said, stepping past her. Laramie followed, frowning at Barbara because she still seemed familiar to him.

"Barbara, who was at—" Clifton asked, entering the living room, but he stopped short when he saw Clint and Laramie.

"Two surprises, eh, Clifton?" Clint asked.

"What are you talking about?"

"Seeing me still here, and seeing Laramie Jones alive, I mean."

"I still don't know—"

"Your man talked, Clifton. He told us and the sheriff that you hired him to kill Laramie. What we want to know is why?"

"This is rid—"

Laramie produced his gun at that point and cocked it.

"I want to know the answer to that question real bad, Clifton. What have you got against me?"

"Gary, what the hell is going on here?"

Clifton gave his wife an annoyed look, and then seemed to make a decision.

"You want to know what's going on?" he asked her. "I'll tell you, and I'll tell them." He looked at Laramie and said, "It's her brother."

"Who?" Laramie said.

"Bob?" she asked.

"Broome?" Clint asked, remembering a man named Bob Broome from the poker game.

"What has he got to do with these men?" she asked.

"He's the reason I hired a man to kill you," Clifton told Laramie.

"Bob Broome?" Clint asked again.

"Yes, Bob Broome," Clifton said "My wife's brother, who owns the hardware store."

"What's he got against me?"

"Why don't you ask him?" Clifton said. "I was just doing what I always do, cleaning up after my wife's brother's mess."

"But . . . murder?" Barbara said. "My brother wouldn't stand for such—"

"Your brother is spineless enough to stand for anything, as long as he didn't have to actually do it," Clifton said. He turned to Clint and Laramie and said, "Go to the hardware store and ask him."

At that point there was another knock at the door.

"That'll be the sheriff," Clint said. "We'll let him in and be on our way."

"Clint," Barbara said. "My brother—"

"Why don't you come along, Barbara," he suggested. "You're entitled to find out what's been going on."

The three of them left, admitting the sheriff, who held his gun on Clifton.

"Let's take a walk to the jail, Clifton," the lawman said. "There's a friend of yours waiting for you there."

•   •   •

When the door to the hardware store opened, Bob Broome looked up. He saw Clint Adams and Laramie Jones, and groped for the gun under the counter. As he came up with it, he saw his sister.

"Barbara!"

"Bob, don't!" she shouted.

Both Clint and Laramie had their guns out, and if Broome made the slightest wrong move, they would have shot him.

"Put it down!" she shouted.

"Barbara—" he said, lowering the gun. "Jesus."

Clint moved forward very quickly and plucked the gun from his hand. He tucked it into his belt, then holstered his own. Laramie joined him at the counter while Barbara Clifton hurried to join her brother on the other side.

"What's it all about, Broome?" Clint Adams asked. "Why do you want this man dead?"

"Bob, what's he talking about?" Barbara Clifton asked. "What's going on?"

Broome stared at Clint and then at Laramie saying, "Don't you know?"

"No," Laramie said, "I don't know, but I damned well want to."

"But . . . how could you not know?"

"He can't remember," Clint said. "He's got amnesia."

"He's got what?"

"He can't remember anything about his past."

Broome gaped at both of them, and then said, "Oh, my God," and started laughing.

TWENTY-SEVEN

By nightfall Clifton, Broome, and the hired gun were all languishing in Laramie's jail. Clint and Laramie were sitting in Laramie's smaller saloon, because Clifton's was closed for business.

Laramie was brooding into his beer, obviously thinking about what Bob Broome had told them. Once he was in a cell, he suddenly got the urge to talk. . . .

"I was afraid you'd recognize me," Broome said to Laramie.

"Where do we know each other from?"

"You really don't know?"

"No, I don't," Laramie said. Clint had listened, preferring to let the two men hash it out.

"We were in the war together. You couldn't have been more than eighteen at the time."

"The war?"

"The Civil War?"

Clint looked at Laramie, who was looking puzzled. It had never dawned on Clint that among Laramie's lost memories, he wouldn't recall something like the Civil War.

"In fact, we hadn't seen each other since the war until you showed up here that time."

"What was wrong with that?" Laramie asked. "Were we friends?"

"Not really, but we did have something in common."

"What?"

It was then that Clint noticed a crafty glint come into Bob Broome's eyes.

"We were both traitors."

"What?"

"We both worked against the South, friend," Broome said. "We worked as Union spies."

"But . . . I was only eighteen."

"That don't matter. We both knew what we were getting into."

"But . . . why?"

"Why else? For money. I took mine and came out here where my sister lived, and started a business. You went back home to Atlanta. I became somebody in this town, and then you showed up and threatened it all."

"I don't understand," Laramie said, and Clint sympathized. His head must have been spinning.

"Laramie, if you had revealed to anyone here in town how Broome got the money to start his business, it would have hurt his reputation. Nobody likes a traitor, no matter which side he betrayed."

"And that's me, huh?" Laramie said. "That's the real me. A traitor?"

"Laramie—" Clint said, but the younger man turned on his heel and stalked out of the cell. Seconds later Clint heard the front door open and slam.

"We only have your word that this is true," Clint said to Broome.

Broome looked at Clint and said, "Why would I lie?"

"To hurt the man who has now caused you to be revealed."

Broome did not reply.

"Now tell me, what's his real name?" Clint asked.

"I . . . can't remember."

"You'll tell me—" Clint said, and was advancing on the man when the sheriff entered.

"I won't have that in my jail, Adams," the sheriff said. "You could pull it in the livery, but not in my jail."

"Sheriff—"

"You won't touch this man in my jail."

Clint glared at the sheriff, then past him at Bob Broome, who had a smug look on his face.

"Don't look so satisfied, Broome," Clint said. "Remember, you're finished in this town."

Clint left without looking at Clifton and his gunman, who were sharing the same cell. . . .

Now Clint sat and watched Laramie brood.

"Laramie, we only have his word about the war," Clint reminded him.

"Why would he lie?" Laramie asked. "I've come all this way to find out that I am a traitor."

"We haven't found out anything about your personal life, though. We don't even know your name."

"The name of a traitor," Laramie said, standing up. "I don't want to know."

"Where are you going?"

"Back to my hotel room. I'll be leaving town in the morning, Clint. You can go back to Texas, or wherever. Thanks for your help."

"Laramie—" Clint said, but there was no consoling the man. Clint settled back into his seat and started to brood into his own beer, when the batwing doors opened and Mona came in.

"I've been looking for you."

"I've been here."

"I . . . I'm locked out of the saloon. I thought that maybe . . . you might—"

"Sure," Clint said, standing up. "My room is your room. To tell you the truth, I could use the company."

TWENTY-EIGHT

Clint tried to empty his mind and enjoy Mona. She was sympathetic when they arrived at his room.

"Would you rather talk for a while?" she asked. "Or go to sleep?"

"How could I stay in this room with a woman as beautiful as you and just talk?" he asked. "Or sleep? That is, unless you want to."

"I want you, Clint," she said, "but we'll do whatever you want. I don't know exactly what happened, today, but I know you're not happy about it."

"Maybe we'll talk about it . . . after," he said, taking her into his arms.

Laramie lay on the bed in his room, staring at the ceiling, trying to remember when he was eighteen. What could have made an eighteen-year-old turn against his own people? Could it have been just money? And was it known in his home—wherever that was—that he was a traitor? How did his family—if he had any—feel about that?

He hadn't even asked Broome what his name was, or where his home was, but did he want to know those things now? How could he bear to go back "home" now, knowing what he did about himself?

It would have better to leave it all unknown, he thought, turning on his side.

"It would have been better. . . ."

Mona's clothes seemed to melt off her, and then she was gloriously naked. Her breasts were high and firm, with large pink nipples. She helped Clint out of his clothes, then took hold of his swollen penis and led him by it to the bed.

He lay on his back and she loomed over him. She kissed his nipples and rubbed her breasts against him, her long, blond hair hanging over him, working a wet path down to his turgid penis, which she then took into her mouth.

She moaned as she worked on him, encircling his penis at the base with one hand, fondling his balls with the other, working her mouth wetly up and down the length of him. She wanted to make him forget what was making him unhappy, and from the sounds he was making, from the way he lifted his hips up off the bed, she felt sure she was doing just that.

As he began to spurt into her mouth, Clint's mind went totally blank, and he know nothing but the searing pleasure of Mona's greedy mouth milking him for more; pleasure and pain mixing as it did when the pleasure was so intense. . . .

Laramie tossed and turned in his sleep.

The dream was back.

The sharp bite of the whip. . . .

The hot sun. . . .

But there was no fog in the man's face now and his back was not to the sun.

See it, Laramie told himself. This is your dream. See the face.

He looked up as the man paused with the whip and there, plain as day, was the man's face, laughing. . . .

Laramie sat bolt upright in bed, the sweat rolling down his face. Finally, he knew who the man was who had whipped him, almost to death, and he knew he could not allow that act to go unavenged, no matter what else he had learned.

He stood up, strapped on his gun and left the room.

"How awful," Mona said after Clint had finished telling her the story. "It must be terrible not to remember your past, and then to find out about it like that . . . . He must feel just terrible."

"He does," Clint said, "but I'm not sure I believe Broome."

"You think he lied?"

"I think he saw a chance to hurt Laramie, and he took it."

"But that's even worse. To lie to someone who has no way of knowing whether or not you're telling the truth."

"Yes," Clint said. "It is worse."

He sat up.

"Where are you going?"

"I'm going to go over to the jail and talk to Broome. There are still some things he can tell us."

"Like what?"

"Like Laramie's real name, like where his home is—wait a minute," Clint said, stopping with one leg in and one out of his pants.

"What is it?"

"He did tell us where Laramie's home is. He said that after the war, and after they got paid, Laramie went home to Atlanta, and Broome came here."

"Atlanta, Georgia?"

"That's the only one I know of."

"Are you going to go there?"

"If I get what I want from Broome, and if I can convince Laramie that's it worth going back," Clint said, strapping on his gun. "Mona, you stay here and get some sleep."

"Will you be leaving tomorrow?"

"I think so. You can keep this room until you find someplace to stay."

"I'm not worried about that," she said. "I'll just be sorry to see you leave."

He cupped her chin in his hand and said, "Get some sleep. I'll be back in a while and then we'll have the rest of the night to say good-bye."

TWENTY-NINE

Clint left the hotel and walked across the quiet main street of Laramie. He had briefly considered stopping at Laramie's room and talking him into accompanying him but thought better of it. Maybe it would be better to simply approach him when he had all the information about his past.

What was important now was figuring out a way to get the sheriff to let him question Broome—alone.

Clint reached the sheriff's office and peered in the window to see if the sheriff was there. He didn't think the man would leave the office unmanned, but maybe he'd drafted a temporary deputy for the job. He was puzzled when he saw no one inside, but then he saw the steaming cup of coffee on top of the desk and looked closer. That was when he saw the man's legs on the floor behind the desk.

Clint entered the office and hurried to the desk. Lying behind it was the sheriff. He had a lump on his head, but the skin had not been broken, and he was breathing all right. Fearing a jail break—maybe engineered by Gary Clifton's friends—Clint drew his gun and opened the door to the cell block.

"I'm going to kill you whether you stand up or not, Clifton," he heard Laramie say, and then he knew what had happened.

"Laramie!" he called.

Laramie was standing on front of Clifton's cell, pointing his gun at the man. Clifton's gunman was crouched in the other corner, and Broome was watching with fascination from his cell, probably wondering if he would be next.

Upon hearing Clint's voice, Laramie did not turn around and did not lower the gun.

"Get out of here, Clint," Laramie said. "I'm going to kill Clifton."

"Why? Why Clifton and not Broome?"

"Broome's a coward," Laramie said. "He's not worth killing. Clifton is the one who did his dirty work for him. Remember that dream?"

"I remember."

"Well, I had it again tonight, and I did what you told me. I saw the face—his face!"

"He's crazy!" Clifton said. "What the hell is he talking about? What dream?"

"You were the man who whipped me, Clifton.

You're the man who cost me my memory, my past life."

"Not much of a life, if you ask me," Clifton said.

Laramie cocked the hammer back on his gun.

"Stop him!" Clifton shouted.

"Laramie, don't!"

"Get out of here, Clint!"

"Laramie, I came here to question Broome, to find out your name and your home, so we could go there and find out if he's telling the truth. It's the only way."

"It's too late."

"It's not too late, but it will be if you kill Clifton. Listen to me. Broome is lying to you!"

"I'm not lying!"

Clint pointed his gun at Broome and cocked the hammer for effect.

"I don't agree with Laramie, Broome. I think you deserve to die, and there's only one way you can save your life."

"How?"

"You already said that Laramie lived in Atlanta, Georgia, right?"

"That's right."

"Now tell me his name. Answer that question, and you live. It's as easy as that."

Broome stared at Clint, wetting his lips, and then decided that Clint was telling the truth. He would kill him if he didn't answer.

"All right, all right," Broome said. "His name was Henry LaSalle."

"Henry LaSalle?" Clint asked. The name did not

match the man he knew—but then Laramie Jones was not truly Henry LaSalle. That man was gone.

"The LaSalles were a very prominent family in Georgia, Adams. They're not going to like it if this man goes back there. They were disgraced when he turned traitor—"

"That remains to be seen."

"Believe me—"

"That's just the problem, Broome," Clint said, lowering his gun. "I don't believe you."

He did believe him about the name, though.

"Does that name sound familiar, Laramie?"

"LaSalle," Laramie said thoughtfully. "There is something about it. . . ."

"Put that gun down, Laramie. Tomorrow we'll head for Georgia and find out the truth, once and for all. At least now we know exactly where to look. Don't ruin it now!"

"The sheriff—"

"I'll fix it with the sheriff. Come on, Laramie, make the right decision."

There was a tense moment when everyone in the room remained silent, and then Laramie eased the hammer down and lowered the gun.

"Good," Clint said, holstering his own gun. "Now get back to the hotel and I'll square things with the sheriff."

Laramie nodded, holstered his gun and started to walk out. Before he left, though, he looked at Clint and said, "Thanks."

"Thank me when it's all over."

Laramie left, and Clint turned to follow him, but

was stopped by Bob Broome's voice.

"Adams!"

"What do you want?"

"I'm going to help you."

"You mean more than you already have? To what do I owe the pleasure?"

"Just listen to me. Taking that man—LaSalle, Jones, whatever—back to Atlanta isn't going to be healthy for either one of you."

"And why is that?"

"We weren't alone, him and me, in taking money from the Union. There were others, and they didn't leave Georgia like I did. They stayed and made their lives there. If you two show up, they're liable to not take it very well."

"You mean as well as you?"

"They're bigger than me, Adams," Broome said ominously. "Mark my words. The two of you go back there, you're as good as dead."

Clint turned his back on Broome and went out to the main office. He didn't know what he was going to tell the sheriff, but it had to counteract whatever the prisoners had told him.

It was going to have to be a hell of a whopping lie.

Clint returned to the hotel after mollifying the sheriff with a story of an attempted jailbreak. Naturally the men in the cell would tell a different story if someone had tried to break them out. Clint felt sure that even if the sheriff didn't believe him, he was confused enough for the moment. By the time he straightened it out, they'd be long gone.

He slid into bed next to Mona, who was sleeping peacefully, and even though he'd said that they would have the night to say good-bye, he couldn't bring himself to wake her.

He lay awake next to her, staring at the ceiling and thinking about what Broome had told him. How much of what this man said was lie, and how much was truth, he wondered.

There may very well have been a reason that he didn't want Laramie/LaSalle to return to Atlanta, Georgia, but the only way he and Clint were going to find out the truth was by going there.

Laramie needed the truth. The way it stood now, he was no better off and possibly worse off than when he knew nothing. It had to be settled, one way or another, or it would haunt him the rest of his life.

Mona woke Clint the next morning, scolded him for not waking her when he returned, then made him pay for it with a long session of sex, in every position imaginable. She said it was her way of making sure he'd never forget her.

Mona left the hotel when Clint went to Laramie's room to awaken him. As it turned out Laramie was already awake and had his gear ready to go.

"Breakfast first," Clint said.

"How are we going to get to Georgia?" Laramie asked.

"We'll discuss that after leaving this town," Clint said, thinking of the sheriff.

Breakfast was a quiet meal, and Clint took the opportunity to think about the people he'd met in Laramie. He would never find out why Susan Bell was so desperate to hire him, or how it would have been to bed her. It was too bad she had passed out that night, but on the other hand, he wouldn't have made love to Mona.

Then there was Barbara Clifton. What would happen to her now that her husband and brother were in trouble? She could always keep the saloon open and run it, but somehow Clint didn't see her as a saloon owner. In fact, he didn't know how he saw her. He only knew that he felt sorry for her.

Mona was probably the only person he'd met in town that he liked, and he'd already said good-bye to her.

After breakfast Laramie said, "We'll need supplies."

"It's too early," Clint said. "We'll travel light and stock up at the next town."

They walked to the livery and saddled their own horses.

"Clint," Laramie said.

"What?"

"Thanks for last night."

"You said that already."

"No, but I mean—you saved me from making a big mistake, and you're right. There's still a lot I have to find out about myself."

"Well, that's what we're going to do, kid. Find it all out. From there you can decide if you want to go back to whatever your old life was, or just continue on as Laramie Jones."

"That's going to be a difficult decision."

"And one that you'll have to make on your own. I can get you there, but after that I can't help you."

"I know that," Laramie said. "You're doing enough. I can't—"

"Don't start thanking me again. Let's hit the trail."

As they rode out of town Clint still wasn't sure how they were going to get to Atlanta, Georgia, but one way or the other they'd get there because the truth was waiting for them.

THIRTY

Clint and Laramie waited while Duke was unloaded from the stock car at the train station in Atlanta, Georgia. Since Laramie was not in the least attached to his horse, they had sold it before boarding the train.

"I've never ridden on a train before," Laramie said, then amended the statement. "I mean, that I know of."

"What did you think?"

"I never would have thought anything could go so fast."

Clint, of course, had ridden the iron horse many times, and even regaled Laramie with stories such as his ride on the gambling train, Hell-on-Wheels,[1] when

1. THE GUNSMITH #54: HELL ON WHEELS.

he had ended up solving a murder.

"It must be wonderful to have all those memories," Laramie said, and after that statement, Clint stopped telling him stories. The man was depressed enough without having someone else's memories thrown in his face.

With Duke in hand, Clint asked the whereabouts of the livery stable.

"There's a lot of them hereabouts," the conductor said. "After all, Atlanta is a big city. They really built it up after Sherman's march."

Clint simply asked for a reputable stable and received instructions, which he and Laramie followed on foot.

Atlanta was a full-fledged city, with the kind of concrete sidewalks Clint had seen in Denver, Washington, D.C., and New York. He hadn't known what to expect on his first trip to the Deep South—except, of course, for New Orleans. It was late, almost nightfall, and yet the city was still very much alive, and would probably become even more so after dark. Clint had found that true of large cities.

The liveryman was friendly and helpful, and oohed and aahed over Duke.

"Sir, I know many men who would give you a fair price for that horse," the man said.

"He's not for sale,"

"At any price?"

"At any price," Clint said.

"Just so I know what to tell them when they offer," the man said.

"You know what to tell them."

The liveryman, a tall, slender man with freckles and sparse red hair asked, "Are you gentlemen here on business or pleasure?"

"Business," Clint said.

"What sort of business?"

"Family business."

"Are your families from here?"

"My friend's is."

"Ah, what might their name be?"

"You ever hear of the LaSalle family?"

"LaSalle," the man said. "But of course. A very prominent family here in Georgia."

"Do they live here in the city?"

The man frowned and looked at Laramie.

"You don't know where your family lives?"

"His path after the war took him West and he's not been back since," Clint explained. "Could you help us?"

"Of course, sir, of course. The LaSalles have a wonderful home just to the north of the city. You could ride there very easily."

"We will probably do that," Clint said, "but first we'd like to check into a hotel."

"But if this gentleman is a LaSalle, I'm sure his family would insist on putting you up. They are a very pleasant and friendly family."

"I'm sure they are," Clint said, "but I would rather start out at a hotel."

"As you wish. The Jubilee House is within walking distance from here, has large rooms with baths, and a wonderful dining room."

"We appreciate the help," Clint said, "Have you lived here long?"

"I settled here after the war."

"Then you don't know my friend, here?"

"I'm sorry," the man said, "but I have never seen him before."

"But you do know the LaSalle family?"

"Oh, yes, very well. Is your friend a cousin of the LaSalles?"

Clint decided to ignore the question.

"Well, we'd better get going," he said, "Again, thank you for the help."

"My pleasure, sir, and rest assured I shall take good care of this fine horse."

"I know you will."

After they walked away, Laramie said, "Why didn't you let me do some talking. That man probably thinks I'm dumbstruck from the war."

"That's fine. Let him think that for now. Better that than to let everyone know that you've got amnesia."

The hotel was a four-story structure made of brick, with huge pillars and a remarkably clean facade. The inside was also spotless.

"What's this going to cost?" Laramie wondered.

"With any luck we won't be here for long. Or would you rather stay in another, less extravagant part of town?"

"Are you kidding? I've never had a bathtub right in my room before. You suppose they have girls to fill them up for you?"

"We can always ask."

They approached the desk, and the clerk looked up from whatever it was he had been finding so interesting.

"Can I help—you," he said, and Clint caught the catch in his throat as plain as day.

He recognized Laramie, and that recognition was making him nervous.

"We'd like two rooms."

"Certainly, sir. Please, just sign in."

Clint signed in for both himself and Laramie, then reversed the book for the clerk to read.

"Ah, Mister—"

"Adams, Clint Adams."

"And Mister, er, Laramie Jones?"

"That's correct."

"Would you like rooms next to one another, sir?"

"If it's no trouble," Clint said.

"It's no trouble at all, sir. Here are your keys. Would you like someone to carry—"

"We can carry our own gear, thank you."

"As you wish, sir. Please, have a pleasant evening."

Clint assured him that they would try.

On the way upstairs Laramie said, "He knew me."

"He sure did."

"Then let's question him."

"No, let him report to whoever and we'll see what happens."

As it turned out, they had boys who filled the tub for them, but the bath was welcome, nevertheless. Afterward, they met in the dining room for dinner.

"What do we do now?" Laramie asked. "Just ride up to the house?"

"I don't see any other way," Clint said. "You'd know soon enough if you were truly a LaSalle that way. We'll do it in the morning though. I'm curious to see what's going to happen here tonight."

Laramie fell silent, and then said, "I'm scared, Clint. Not about tonight, but—"

"About tomorrow. I don't blame you, Laramie—or should I start calling you Henry?"

"Henry?" Laramie said, making a face. "Let's leave it Laramie for now, even though I like it a lot less, now that I've seen the town."

"Can't say as I blame you for that, either."

"I can't believe it," Laramie said. "After all this time I'm going to find out if I have parents, brothers and sisters, a wife and children—"

"Or if Broome was lying and there's nothing here for you," Clint said. "Keep that in mind, as well."

"I will," Laramie said, "I surely will."

After dinner Clint suggested they go back to their rooms and wait.

"For what?" Laramie asked.

"That," Clint said, "is the question. We'll be waiting for the answer."

THIRTY-ONE

The desk clerk had indicated on the register which room key was Clint's and which key was Laramie's. He knew who was in what room, and passed the information on.

The window of Laramie's room was open, and in a hotel of the stature of the Jubilee, the windows didn't squeak when they were opened. Consequently when the man's hand appeared beneath the window and slid it up, the window moved silently. Finally, it was opened completely and a man's leg appeared, then the torso, and then the other leg. He leaned outside then, as if he were saying something, and then backed away from the window to let another man enter.

Both men had guns and produced them as they moved toward the bed. Apparently, though, the guns were a precaution, because one man also took out a knife, which glinted in the moonlight. If they were still in Laramie, a lone shot might go unnoticed, but this was Atlanta, Georgia, and the Jubilee Hotel, to boot. A shot would wake the entire hotel.

The man with the knife started to lean over the figure on the bed when suddenly the wall lamp was turned up. Both men were startled, and stared in surprise at the figure of Clint Adams standing by the door. In the darkness, they had missed him completely in the shadows.

Suddenly a gun came out from beneath the covers of the bed and pressed itself underneath the chin of the man with the knife.

"Throw the knife away, friend," Laramie said.

The desk clerk obeyed, tossing the knife away.

"Now the gun," Laramie said.

"You, too," Clint said to the other man, who had backed toward the window.

There was a tense moment as the two men tried to decide what to do.

"Chance?" the desk clerk asked, obviously looking for guidance.

"Toss it away, Beau," the man called Chance said.

"Chance, I'm not goin' to jail."

"Beau—"

The clerk moved quickly, surprising Laramie. He knocked the prone man's gun aside and started to bring his around. Clint fired one shot, catching the man in the chest. The impact of the bullet drove him back against the wall, but instead of falling, the man tried to raise his gun once again, and Clint fired a second time. This time the men dropped the gun and slid down to the floor, leaving a smear of blood on the wall behind him.

"How about you?" Clint asked the other man.

By way of reply the man tossed his gun to the floor and raised his hands.

Outside in the hall they could hear the commotion as people rushed from their rooms to see what was going on. Clint opened the door wide and a man poked his head in.

"Oh, dear," he said.

"Who are you?" Clint asked.

"The night clerk."

"Does this town have any kind of law?"

"Of course."

"Get some up here, now."

"Yessir."

Clint closed the door as Laramie climbed off the bed and picked up his gun.

"Sorry," he said.

"Don't worry about it. As long as we have this one . . . do you know him?"

Laramie squinted, studying the man and said. "No."

"What?" the man said.

"Amnesia, friend," Clint said. "He can't remember a thing about his life here, but then you didn't know that, did you?"

"Jesus," the man said, shaking his head. He looked like a man who had just made a terrible mistake.

"Chance what?"

"DuBois."

"That figures. What have you got to say for yourself, Chance?"

"Nothing." the man said, composing himself. "I'll wait for the police."

The man was in his early thirties, tall and wide-shouldered. His suit was the kind you would wear to dinner, and not the kind you would climb through windows in.

There was a knock on the door, and when Clint opened it, there was a uniformed policeman there.

"What's going on here, sir?"

"We've caught two intruders, Officer," Clint said as the officer entered.

The policeman spotted the blood on the wall and the man on the floor, and his eyes went wide. Next, he set eyes on the second man, and surprise showed again.

"Mr. DuBois, sir!"

"Hello, Officer."

"You know this man?" Clint asked.

"Well, of course I know him," the policeman said. "We're standing in his hotel."

"What?"

"You heard me. He owns this hotel."

Clint stared at Chance DuBois, who was looking pleased with himself. When he looked back at the officer, he was looking down the barrel of the man's gun.

"I think you had better come with me, sir."

Clint knew he couldn't go against the lawman, so he handed over his gun and said, "Officer, why don't we all go with you. I'm sure we can clear this up."

"My thoughts exactly, sir."

THIRTY-TWO

Chief of Police Ambrose DeWitt sat behind his desk and contemplated Clint Adams.

"I know your reputation, sir, even as far south as this," he said. The man was obese, and had both hands folded and lying on his belly.

"I'm sure this far south it's gotten even more exaggerated than usual," Clint said.

"You must realize that Mr. DuBois is a very important man in Atlanta."

"He tried to kill my friend."

"I have only your word for that."

"And the word of my friend."

"Who by both of your admissions is suffering from an injury to the head."

"Not a recent injury to the head," Clint said. "Amnesia."

"That would still make his testimony suspect in a court of law."

"Look, Chief—"

"Now, Mr. DuBois admits that he might have made a mistake and hired a thief as a desk clerk. He states that you were probably within your rights to shoot the man."

"What does he say about his presence in the room?"

"That he ran upstairs to investigate the shot. He says he knocked on the door and when you opened it, you pulled him in and held your gun on him."

"That doesn't make any sense."

"Neither does the prospect of the owner of a hotel climbing into one of the rooms through a window. Why didn't he just use his master key?"

"He wanted it to look like an intruder killed my friend."

"And that's another thing. Claiming your friend is a LaSalle, one of the most prominent familes in Georgia. By your own admission he has an in—uh, amnesia. How could he claim to be a LaSalle?"

"I told you. He doesn't claim it; someone else told us he was. We came here to investigate it. We checked into the hotel, and the next thing we know, two men climb in the window of his room and try to kill him."

"And you just happen to be there, waiting for them."

"Because I could see that the clerk recognized him. A man who recognized him in Laramie, Wyoming, tried to kill him. I was being cautious."

"Why would Mr. DuBois want to kill him?"

"Because he was afraid that my friend would expose him as—as—"

"As what?"

"Well, possibly a traitor to the Confederacy during the war."

"That's preposterous," the chief said. "Mr. DuBois was a hero."

"Look, Chief, we can settle this fairly easily."

"If you can see an easy way to do this, I'm all for it. Otherwise, I'll have to release Mr. DuBois and your friend, and hold you for a court of enquiry."

"Chief, if you let both of them go and keep me here, my friend will be dead before morning."

"What is your solution?" the chief asked with a sigh that moved his entire stomach.

"Send for someone from the LaSalle family. Have them come in and identify my friend as Henry LaSalle."

"Or not," the chief pointed out.

"Or not."

"I can't do that now," the Chief said.

"Why not?"

"I can't disturb them this late at night. It will have to wait until morning."

"Then hold all three of us until morning."

"I can't hold Mr. DuBois—"

"Sheriff, I'm making a claim against him, and he's making one against me. You can either hold both of us, or let us both go. In the eyes of the law we should both be equal."

Clint was betting—hoping, actually—that the chief was an honest lawman.

After a few moments of deliberation the chief made a face, lifted his buttocks and broke wind, and then said, "Very well. If I let you all go, someone might end up dead. I'll hold you all, and hope it doesn't cost me my job."

"Thank you, Chief. You're an honest man."

"Soon to be an unemployed one."

The chief went to the door and called a man to take Clint back to his cell.

"What happened?" Laramie asked from the next cell.

"We're all being held until someone from the LaSalle family can come in and identify you."

"Then it's going to happen, after all."

"Yes."

"And here," Laramie said, looking over his six-by-six cell. "Where's DuBois?"

"He must be in another cell," Clint said.

"Maybe they let him go."

"I don't think so. The chief struck me as an honest man, but even if they did, as long as someone from the family shows up, we'll be off the hook."

"What happens if they don't identify me?" Laramie said. "What happens if I'm not a LaSalle?"

Clint frowned and said, "If that happens, we might be in a lot of trouble."

THIRTY-THREE

In the morning they were awakened by the sunlight streaming through the small, barred window in each of their cells. Moments later, a guard appeared carrying two trays with breakfast. There were eggs, ham, and biscuits, and it smelled delicious.

"Where did this breakfast come from?" Clint asked as the guard slid his tray in to him.

"From the Jubilee Hotel dining room. They donate breakfasts to the prisoners."

"That figures," Clint said.

They finished breakfast, gave up the trays, then were served lunch and gave those trays up. Still no sign of anyone from the LaSalle family.

"Can I see the chief?" Clint asked the guard.

"The chief's not in."

"Do you know where he went?"

"No."

"Do you know when he'll be back?"

"No."

"You don't know a hell of a lot, do you?"

The guard smiled and said, "No."

"I think we're stuck, Clint," Laramie said. "Your honest chief has double crossed us."

Clint hoped not, but he was starting to believe that Laramie might be right.

They were wondering what they were going to have for dinner when two guards suddenly appeared.

"All right, you two, let's go. The chief wants to see you."

"It's about time," Clint said.

They were led upstairs, but instead of being shown to the chief's office, they were put in another room and seated in straightbacked wooden chairs.

"Now what?" Clint asked one of the guards, but neither man replied.

Finally, a door opened and the chief walked in.

"This way, please," he said to someone behind him.

A man and a woman entered the room behind him. The man was tall, fair-haired with a widow's peak and an angular face. He was in his mid-thirties. The woman was approximately the same age, petite and dark-haired, with a rather plain but nevertheless appealing face. Clint watched both of them closely as they inspected both he and Laramie. The chief's ploy was obvious. Though the differences in Clint and Laramie's age would be a giveaway, he was still giving them a choice of two faces instead of one to identify as a LaSalle.

The man looked at Clint and Laramie with the same vacant look on his face, but the woman looked from Clint to Laramie, frowned, studied Laramie more carefully, and then suddenly gasped.

Clint looked at Laramie and there was a strange look on his face, as well. He was staring at the woman strangely, and then half rose from his chair. A guard moved and the chief waved him away.

"Melanie?" Laramie said. "Mel?"

"Henry!" the woman cried, and rushed into Laramie's arms, crying into his chest.

"Mr. Fielding?" the chief said.

"Chief, this man is obviously my brother-in-law, Henry LaSalle. I don't know where he's been all these years, but he's back now, and I want him out of your jail."

"Of course, sir."

"And my friend," Laramie/LaSalle said.

"And his friend," Fielding said, and the chief nodded. Apparently, the LaSalle name—through this Fielding—held more weight than even Chance DuBois.

Fielding approached brother and sister and said to Laramie, "Welcome home, Henry."

He held out his hand and Laramie took it, keeping his other arm around his "sister." He looked over her head at Clint, who could see the confusion on his face. It would probably take a long time for him to deal with the fact that he had found his family.

THIRTY-FOUR

Once "Henry LaSalle" entered his old home, the memories seemed to come back one by one. He had left behind no wife and children because he had only been eighteen when he left. He *had* left behind a mother and father, but they had died. His sister, Melanie, had married a man named John Fielding, and they took over the family home. The Fielding name was a powerful one on its own, but combined with the LaSalle name it was even more formidable.

They spent the night at the house, and Laramie and Clint were the first ones down for breakfast.

"How was it last night?" Clint asked. He had turned in early, while Henry and Melanie had sat up, talking.

"We sat up half the night, Clint. It's all come back to me now, except for one or two things."

"Tell me about it."

"Both Broome and DuBois were in my unit in the war, and apparently—I can't recall how—I found out that they were working for the Union for money. They didn't kill me, but they did threaten my family if I returned to Atlanta and exposed them."

"Your family was a powerful one, Lar—uh, Henry."

"I know that, but I was young then. I thought I was doing the honorable thing by leaving them and traveling west. I traveled for a few years, doing odd jobs, until I got to Laramie and saw Broome."

"After he and Clifton got through with you, Henry LaSalle had disappeared."

"To be replaced by Laramie Jones."

"And now?"

"I don't know. I still feel like Laramie, but I remember Henry now. He was a little foolish, perhaps, but all in all he wasn't a bad sort."

Clint smiled and Laramie/Henry said, "What are you smiling at?"

"You've even got a touch of a southern accent, now."

"I guess I didn't lose it entirely."

"Congratulations, Henry, on not being a traitor and a spy."

"Thank you . . . but DuBois was. What do I do about that?"

"That's up to you," Clint said. "You can expose

him, or you can leave him be. I don't think he's a danger to you, not now that you're a LaSalle again. Make a deal with him, turn him in, but decide on your own . . . Henry."

It was then that Henry saw Clint's saddlebags and rifle leaning against the wall.

"Are you leaving?"

"Yes. Your brother-in-law had Duke brought over last night. I thought I'd ride through the south a ways, maybe all the way back west."

"Now?"

"Well, after breakfast," Clint said. "I want to leave you and your sister to get reacquainted, Henry, and I've got to get headed back to where I belong."

"Clint, I don't know how to thank you."

They shook hands and Clint said, "If you forget Laramie Jones, do me a favor?"

"What."

"Remember me."

Henry LaSalle smiled and said, "Deal."

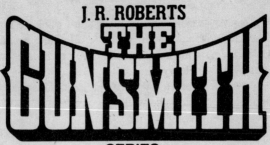

J. R. ROBERTS
THE GUNSMITH

SERIES